LENNIE GRACE

Bite Sized Horrors: The Complete Series

Contents

I

81 Horror Drabbles

Book 1

The Monster Will Get You

"Don't go down there!"

"Melissa!" I tugged away from her. "It's just the basement! I have to get the Halloween decorations."

"Mommy! The monster will get you!"

"Don't be silly!"

"They will! They hate noise. You're loud!"

"Am not!"

"Ssshhh!" she insisted.

I stomped downstairs.

I tried finding the light switch. No luck. Shrugging, I moved into the dark. My arm bumped a stack of boxes. They fell with a BOOM!

Dang. Maybe I *was* loud.

"Sssshhh!"

Trembling, I watched as a grinning, glowing face came out of the dark.

"Too loud!"

"Huh?"

"Ssshhh!" It hissed.

Then the monster attacked.

The Aliens' Lefterovers

There's a picture of my lasted kill on the news. A sweet little boy, only five years old. The captain below the reporter reads *Child goes missing from park.*

I chuckle to myself as the reporter lists facts and asks anyone with information to contact the police.

Searching won't do any good.

He didn't run away, and he didn't get lost. It doesn't matter how frantically the parents and everyone else in the neighborhood searches.

They'll never find him.

There's nothing left to find.

That's the thing about my pet aliens. When they're hungry, they never leave leftovers for tomorrow.

The Worst Meal of the Day

I swim through the river, enjoying the feeling of cool water flowing around me.

I'm hungry.

I search for food. I hope I find something good.

And I do. It's strange. Wiggly. I swim closer and bit it. It's soft and delicious. But inside, there's something stabby. It jabs my mouth.

It hurts!

I try to swim. I'm not hungry anymore.

But then the thing in my mouth rips me up out of the water.

I gasp, my gills flapping. Too bright! Too loud! I'm terrified.

"Check it out!"

My terror increases. Humans! I wiggle, but can't escape.

I'm food.

Losing the Game

There was no food. The electricity was out. Even the water was running out.

Someone had to get more supplies.

Someone had to go outside.

But that meant risking the mutants, and we had no weapons. My friends and I sat in the dark basement.

Hungry.

Thirsty.

Dirty.

Scared.

In the beam of a dying flashlight, we played rock paper scissors to see who it'd be.

I lost.

My friends looked away. I didn't need to read minds to know what they were thinking.

I was the weakest one.

I would fail.

In a way, we all lost the game.

The Night Shift

The other gas station employees hate working the night shift. I don't mind. I'm a night owl.

The door dings. A man comes in. He has a ski mask and a gun.

A robber? Fun!

"Give me the money, or I shoot!"

"I don't think so."

He points the gun at me. "Now!"

"Nope."

Bang!

I stumble. There's a bloody hole in my forehead. It hurts, but I'm alright.

I grin at him.

"What the fuck!?"

I grin wider, displaying my fangs. "Do you still want to try and take the money?"

"What... are you?"

"I'm thirsty," I say happily.

Like An Adult

It was such a stupid fear. Connor knew that. So why did he always check under the bed for monsters before going to sleep? There wasn't anything lurking under there. And Conner wasn't a baby.

Determined to stop the childish habit, Conner did not check under the bed that night.

There.

Weren't.

Any.

Monsters!

He fell asleep quickly, feeling very proud of himself. Like an adult.

He woke up to the feeling of someone watching him. Yawning, he turned on the lights. A clown with glowing eyes stood over him.

"You shove have checked for monsters," the clown told him.

Campfire Stories

"And then… when they got home… There was a rusty hook on the door. Just… like… this!"

Everyone squealed as Beth pulled a plastic hook from her hoodie pocket. The kind from cheap Halloween costumes.

"Stop it! You *know* I hate ghost stories!"

"Don't be a wuss, Kayla," Josh said. "We're camping. We gotta tell scary stories!"

"I don't like it!"

"They're just stories!" Beth laughed. "There's not *really* any monsters or murderers here."

"I know! But-"

"Hey," Josh interrupted. "Where'd Mikey go?"

"Maybe he had to pee?"

"Mikey?" Kayla called timidly.

Somewhere out in the dark, Mikey began screaming.

The Cries for Help

The house burns down around me. I want to run.

I can't. I'm a firefighter. Someone is down in the basement, screaming for help.

For one second, I hesitate at the top of the basement stairs, knowing how dangerous this is.

"Help! Please!" someone sobs. It sounds like a child.

I take a deep breath and run down.

I search, but no one is there. I was certain I heard someone.

I turn to go back. At the top of the stairs, is a little girl made of fire.

She giggles as she slams the door and locks me inside.

The Human's Dinner

I'd worked hard making dinner for my pet. But she didn't want it.

"Eat up!" I encouraged.

She didn't move from the corner of her cage.

"What's wrong?" my mate asked.

"She's not eating!" I pointed at the meal with my tail.

My pet began crying.

"Maybe she doesn't want it?" my mate suggested.

How could she *not* want it? It was her baby cooked in its own blood. This was a great thing, to eat one's firstborn! Everyone did it on our home planet.

"Don't feed her anything else until she eats it," my mate suggested.

"Okay," I agreed.

Seeing the Monster

The monster reached from under the bed. It stroked my arm, its claws irritating my skin.

I shuddered, but I kept my eyes closed.

If I opened them before my alarm went off, the beast would eat me.

"Aren't you going to look at me?" the monster hissed.

"No!"

"Please?"

"No!" The faster I got to sleep, the faster morning would come. Then I would be safe again.

I gasped as claws sank into my arm. My eyes instinctively opened.

The monster loomed above me. I shut my eyes again, but it was too late.

The monster saw me looking.

The Worst Kind of Goodbye

"No! There has to be another way!"

Benny grimaced in pain, one hand clamped over the bite on his arm. His hands were turning green.

Rotted.

Dead.

"You can't leave me!"

"I think I have to, Jake."

Benny was turning. It was my fault. We should've never let the hideout.

He passed me the gun. "Don't let me turn."

"I can't shoot you!"

"And I can't hurt you!"

Slowly, I took the gun. I kissed his cheek. We were both crying.

"I love you," Benny said.

I aimed at his head.

"I love you too."

Then I pulled the trigger.

Getting Ready

Knock-knock!

Tammy tensed.

Knock-knock!

"Tammy!" Justice whined.

Tammy swore in annoyance and called, "just a minute!"

"Hurry up, or we'll be late for the party!"

"Give me five minutes!"

Justice was annoying! Maybe Tammy should kill her later.

"If you're not in the car in exactly five minutes, I'm leaving without you!" Justice threatened.

"Okay!" Tammy hissed. "Be right out!"

She listened as Justice's footsteps faded. The front door opened and closed. She relaxed a little. She didn't like it when Justice hovered. Tammy went back to trying to get her makeup just right.

It was hard without a reflection.

Ice Fishing

I love ice fishing. It's my favorite activity.

Nothing but me, my equipment, a big circle in the ice, and the fish, of course. To me, the frozen lake is heaven. I have fun even when I don't catch anything.

Today though, I'm lucky. I've got three fish already, and I'm about to get a fourth.

I concentrate on bringing it up. It's a big one, and it wants to escape. I won't let it.

I'm having fun. Until the fish is close enough for me to see.

It's not a fish. It's a monster. And its coming for me.

The Giant Monsters

He was sunning himself on a big rock when he was attacked. The big lumbering monster swung a shovel at him.

He tried to slither away, but it was too late. The shovel tore through his back, his stomach, everything. He thrashed in agony as blood pooled across the stone.

Half!

The monster cut him in half!

The world grew dark as he wondered why the monster hurt him.

"Ha! Look! I got the sneaky little bastard!" the monster cheered.

"Mommy! Why'd you kill it! It wasn't doing anything!"

"I had to."

"Why!?"

"Cause that's what you do with snakes."

The Hanging Tree

A long time ago, my home town was part of the old west. Like cowboys and cattle rustlers. We even have a cool old jailhouse.

It's a big tourist attraction.

My favorite part of the tour is the Hanging Tree that's behind the jail. They used to execute criminals there. They kinda still do.

Because one man is still there.

Still hanging.

He must be immortal or something because he's just as alive and kicking as the day they strung him up.

It's gross, but he killed ten people. So he'll stay there until he finally dies.

Whenever that is.

The Worshipped Ones

I never understood why we worshipped them. Sure, they were vampires. But not like the beautiful sparkly ones in my favorite books.

The Worshipped Ones were ugly.

Gross.

Wrong.

I couldn't share those thoughts. Not if I wanted to live.

The other villagers and I watched as the latest sacrifice was pushed through the gate.

He begged for mercy.

The village leader locked the gate. "If you won't worship them, you will feed them."

"Please! Let me in!"

Ignoring him, the leader rang the dinner bell.

As the sunset, the Worshipped Ones awoke. And then began screaming their joyous hunger.

Before the Invasion

They were coming. The Monsters from another universe. She knew what they did to planets.

They destroyed all creatures on them.

Then they colonized.

She couldn't let that happen. As queen, she had a duty to protect her planet.

They didn't have the resources to fight off the invaders.

Trying would make it worse.

There was only one thing to do.

She sat alone in her war room, staring at The Button.

Around her, screens flashed. They were almost here.

She took a deep breath. And pushed The Button.

***

From outer space, the invaders watched as the new planet exploded.

In the Chicken Coop

"Damn it!" I yelled.

"What's wrong?" My wife ran from the house to check on me.

"This!" I held up the mutilated bird. The fourth one this week.

"What'll we do?"

"I'm gonna stop it."

That night, I waited in the chicken coop with a shotgun.

Finally, the door opened.

Something crept inside.

BANG!

The sleeping chickens startled at the gunshot. I ignored them and shone the flashlight at the dead monster.

It was big, hairy. Its head was wolfish. Its body vaguely human.

And it was shrinking.

My gun fell. I began screaming as the monster became my wife.

The Monster Inside Me

Before I slept with him, he told me he was a monster.

I thought he was joking. I said I didn't care. I told him, "Hush. Just kiss me."

So we slept together. We fell asleep in each other's arms. I was happy. I thought he liked me.

But when I woke up, he was gone.

I wasn't alone though.

I was pregnant.

He told the truth. He was a monster.

And so was his baby.

It grew too fast to be human. And it had claws. I could feel it digging. Stronger each day. His baby monster wanted out.

Paying the Troll

The only way across the bridge was to pay. But Jen and her family were broke. It was why they were going to the city.

To find jobs.

The troll stood threateningly in the center of the bridge.

"Please," Jen's father begged. "Let us pass! We'll bring payment soon."

"Now!"

"We have no coin! What else do you want?"

The troll thought. Then he pointed to Jen. "Hungry…"

"You want to *eat* her?"

The troll nodded.

Her father considered it. "Okay."

"Daddy!"

"It's what's best for the family."

Jen's family crossed the bridge, ignoring her screams as she was devoured.

Not My Dog

I always wanted a dog, but Dad wouldn't let me have one. So when I moved out, the first thing I did was adopt a pet.

I was so proud when I brought him home. I opened the crate so he could explore the apartment.

But what came out…

It wasn't my dog.

It was a monster with too many legs and eyes. Blood dripped from a mouth full of razor-sharp teeth.

I backed up, terrified. Did this thing *eat* my dog? I didn't have much time to wonder though. Because the thing was watching me.

And it looked hungry.

Cooking the Competition

Kristin hated her baby brother. He was so loud, boring, annoying, and useless.

But her parents adored him.

They barely paid any attention to her anymore. They only cared about Peter.

Why?!

He wasn't interesting. All he did was scream and poop.

Kristin glared at him. He napped in his crib. She was supposed to watch him while Daddy mowed the lawn and Mommy worked in her office.

Carefully she picked him up and took him to the kitchen. She opened the door to the oven. Smiling, she placed him inside.

Peter slept soundly as she turned the oven on.

Blood on the Road

I think I screamed. I'm not sure. Everyone was screaming. One second everything was normal. A perfect Sunday on a little town's main street.

Then the little boy ran into the road.

Right in the path of the truck.

It was going to fast, and right before the kid bolted, I saw the driver check his phone.

Then the screams started. His dad's screams were the loudest.

The breaks squeal. People kept screaming, but no one knew what to do.

The truck hit him with the most awful noise.

Blood smeared across the road.

And the little boy was still.

My Daughter's Journal

A purple notebook. "KEEP OUT!" written on the cover. My daughter's journal.

I *knew* I shouldn't read it.

But I couldn't resist. I opened it to a random page. Just a peek. I read three sentences.

I stabbed her.

I liked it.

I wanna do it again.

I felt so sick. It *couldn't* be true!

Then I remembered the new stories. A missing girl. Devastated parents.

I put the journal back where I found it. I had to call the police. I turned. And froze.

My daughter stood in the doorway, holding a knife. "You shouldn't read other people's stuff."

School is Torture

I struggle to finish my math test. I have to answer every question. How bad I'm punished depends on how many answers I get wrong.

But a wrong answer is nothing compared to not finishing.

I finish seconds before the buzzer sounds. I can't be relieved yet. The tests have to be graded.

My classmates and I sit in terrified silence as the teacher grades. Halfway through the tests, he looks up.

"Jerry?"

Jerry goes still.

"You missed a question." The teacher pressed the button.

The Punishers come in. They drag Jerry into the punishment room. Then the screaming starts.

The Zookeeper

"You're fired, Kyle," my boss said.

"Why?!"

"You're rude. Insubordination. You half-ass the jobs you hate. Should I keep going?"

"No," I growled.

"Good. Hand over your keys."

I dropped them on her desk.

"You're going to regret this."

She laughed. She actually *laughed* at me losing the job I love. "I doubt that."

Seething, I went home and waited. Once it was dark and the zoo was closed, I went back. I went in using the extra set of keys I'd made.

Methodically, I opened all the cages. Even the lions and tigers.

I told her she'd regret it.

The Haircut

"I love your hair, Beth," Joanne sighed enviously as she brushed her hair.

"You really like it?"

"I love it!" Joanne promised. "It's beautiful." It was true. Her chocolaty hair was thick, wavy, and shiny. The definition of healthy hair.

"Thanks."

Joeanne couldn't see her friend's face, but she knew Beth was blushing. Beth wasn't great with compliments.

"I wish it could have it."

Beth giggled, "Too bad it's attached to me. Otherwise, I'd totally share it."

"Yeah…" Joanne reached for a pair of scissors.

If *that* was all that was stopping Beth from sharing, it could easily be fixed.

The New Dress

Mia smiled as she opened her birthday present. A beautiful blue dress. She smiled and squealed.

"Do you like it?" I asked.

"I love it! This is the exact one I wanted." She hugged it to her chest and leaned into me. I beamed as she kissed me. "You are officially the best boyfriend ever."

"Really?"

"Of course!" Mia took it to the mirror, holding it up to admire. "Are you sure you can afford it?"

"Sure I can." It was expensive, but I didn't buy it. The girl I killed bought it. All I paid for was dry cleaning.

The Firer Starter

Last week, four people died in a house fire. A mom, dad, and two little boys.

Everyone blamed the fire on the nanny. They said she was having an affair with the dad. That she was jealous of the mom.

So she set fire to the house. She wanted to kill her and take over her role, her life.

Everyone said she was nuts.

She denied it, of course. She swore she didn't start the fire.

But no one believed her.

I'm glad they didn't. While everyone is focused on her, I can choose another family to set on fire.

Morning Gardening

The morning was beautiful as I helped my wife with backyard chores.

"So what do I do?"

"Can you weed the flowerbeds?"

I nodded and started working, carefully pulling up bits of grass. The last weed was huge. I tugged hard.

It came out with a ripping noise and tons of dirt. "Whoo!" My grin vanished as I noticed something. Something that didn't match the soil. I leaned closer, shoving aside dirt.

"Becky!"

"What?"

"Hand... Body! In the dirt!"

She laughed. "I know."

"What?!"

"Yep. I put it there."

"What!?"

"Did you *really* think our neighbor died of old age?"

So Not Funny

Dark.

It was too dark down here.

He wanted out, but there was no way to do that. The coffin was nailed shut, locked up tight.

He pounded against the wood, screaming for help.

No one heard him.

"Help!" he wailed. "Please!"

No one came for him.

He sobbed, gasping for air that was running out. He was trapped. He was going to die.

No one knew he was down here, very much alive, and trapped beneath six feet of dirt.

"Help," he whispered softly.

He was so stupid! Why did he ever think faking his death would be funny?

Lunch With Friends

I love my friends. Except for Karen.

She's the worst.

I used to like her. Now I hate her. Why are we still friends?

Today, my friends and I are at a cafe. It's a long wait for food. Karen takes it out on our waiter.

He apologizes. She calls him stupid. She demands to see the manager.

I snap.

"Shut up, Karen!" I scream. I grab a plate. It shatters over her head. She seems surprised.

I punch her stupid face. She falls. Her head smacks a table.

"Shut up, Karen," I mutter as blood turns blond hair red.

Online Shopping Stinks

There's a knock at the door. I answer to find a delivery person.

"Thank you!" I say and take my package inside.

I set the box on the kitchen table and take a picture. I send it to my best friend with a message. *My new shoes are here!*

I set my phone aside and tear into the package. Inside is a shoebox.

Yay! I've been waiting so long!

My smile dims a little. Something stinks.

I shrug and tug the lid off.

I almost vomit as I see what's making the stink. Inside the shoes are rotting human feet.

My Pet Mouse

The mouse in my hands was so small and helpless. *So* in my power. Just a squeeze, a little pressure, and I could end its life.

The thought made me feel powerful.

It squeaked and tried to escape my grasp. I wondered if it could sense the danger it was in. Mice had such small brains after all.

I smiled as I closed my hands around the mouse and squeeze. The tiny heartbeat stopped. Fragile little bones crunch and little organs squish. I dropped the mouse next to the other dead ones.

I was out of pets.

I needed more.

The Handcuffs

I wake up to pain, smoke, and fire. I gasp as I take in the sight of my bedroom filling with orange, red, and black.

I scream and try to get up. Something jerks me back down. The handcuffs my wife surprised me with for our anniversary.

I'm cuffed to the headboard.

I'm trapped.

I screamed louder. "Help!"

The flames spread over the wallpaper, the carpet, the mattress. I'm sweating, burning. I scream and struggle. But there's no way to escape.

Where's my wife? Where is Marian?!

I find her in the doorway, smiling smugly as she shuts the door.

Dumped

I hate him. He broke up with me. "It's over," he said.

He ruined my life. He *left* me.

Nobody leaves me.

Nobody.

I decide when a relationship was over.

Not him.

I made sure my gun was loaded as I watched him from the bushes. I could see him through the window. He was cleaning. Any second now, he'd come outside to take out the trash.

The waiting was torture.

Finally, the door opened. He walked down the driveway, humming to himself.

I rose from my hiding place. I raised the gun.

BANG!

"*Now* it's over," I said smugly.

The Lab Rat

He didn't know why he'd been taken from his home. His kidnappers knew of course. But they weren't sharing that information.

Whenever he begged to know what they wanted, they told him, "Lab rats don't need details."

That was how they thought of him.

Not as a person.

A lab rat.

An animal.

From his cage, he watched his kidnappers eat breakfast.

They had waffles.

He had water once a day. Nothing else.

Lab rat they called him.

Maybe they wanted to see how long he'd live without food.

His stomach rumbled. He was so hungry.

He wouldn't last long.

Happy Hills

Happy Hills Retirement Home. Everyone thought the place was great. The residents, the workers, even the relatives who came to visit.

Except for Nick.

He *hated* this place. It stank of pee and old people. This was a miserable place, full of gross old people waiting to die.

The only thing that made Nick's job bearable was helping them die faster.

It was so easy. Just a pillow over the face and everyone assumed they died of old age.

But it wasn't.

It was Nick. The secret made him feel powerful.

Happy Hills, Nick thought. *A great place to die.*

The Boss

His boss screamed at him, her voice like nails on a chalkboard. He wasn't sure what he'd done wrong this time. Sometimes he thought she just liked yelling. Maybe it made her feel important.

It was okay though. Let her scream. Soon, he'd take her away to his cabin in the woods. Then she'd realize just how unimportant she really was.

She had no family, no friends. No one to miss her.

It'd be fun to hear her screaming in pain for once and not anger. Soon she'd have a real reason to be mad at him.

He couldn't wait.

Hearts and Hosting

Quinn couldn't believe he let himself be talked into this.

Him?

Host a dinner party? It was crazy! Quinn was a pretty… Limited cook.

And he was pretty sure his friends wouldn't like his meals.

He tried telling them he didn't want to host, but everyone insisted.

"It's your turn, Quinn!" Vance had said. "Just make whatever. It'll be great!"

Quinn looked doubtfully at the oven. Dang it. He should've just ordered a pizza. Instead, he panicked and made his favorite meal.

Quinn hoped the group liked children's hearts as much as he did. If not, they'd be tomorrow's dinner.

Morning Coffee

He smiled as the worker passed him his coffee and muffin through the drive-thru window.

"Here you go!" she was amazingly perky for seven in the morning. "Have a nice day."

"Thank you," he said. He rolled up his window and drove off. A mile or two down the road, he took his first sip of coffee.

He frowned, glancing at the cup.

It tasted funny.

When he got to work, he took the lid off to check his drink. Did they accidently give him someone else's?

His stomach twisted as he realized what his cup was filled with.

Blood.

Screen Time

"Honey? Selena?"

I glanced up from my phone. "What is it?" I snapped. "I'm busy!"

"The baby needs her bath, and I just got called into work. Can you do it?"

"But I'm busy!" I protested, but he didn't seem to notice.

"Great! Thanks!" he dumped the baby in my arms, kissed me, and rushed out.

Gross. I hated bathing the kid as much as I hated my screen time being interrupted.

I took the baby to the bathroom. I filled the tub with cold water. Then I tossed her in.

That would teach my husband not to interrupt me.

Keeping Me Away

It was too dark in here. Too cold, too cramped. I hated it more than I hated my parents. And that was saying something. I tried to get more comfortable, but it was hard with so little room.

For the hundredth time, I beat on the walls of my wooden prison.

"Help!" I screamed.

No one answered.

And no one came to help.

"Help," I repeated, but this time it was a weak sob instead of a scream. "Please… Help…"

I knew my parents didn't like my boyfriend, but I never thought they'd bury me to keep me from him.

The Jacket

He works alone in his basement. He's making his own clothing. It's his favorite hobby. Today, he's working on something exciting. Something new. Something unique.

He's designing a jacket made from human skin.

His wife brings him lunch around noon.

"How's the project going?" she asks.

He shows her his drawings. "What do you think?"

She kisses him. "It's beautiful. Have you picked someone? The source material has to be just right."

He eagerly pulled a picture up on his phone. "It's that bitch from your book club. I thought she'd be good."

His wife kissed him again. "She's perfect."

Bite-sized Pieces

I put earplugs in to drown out the screams of my dinner. It didn't work very well. So I added noise-canceling headphones.

That was a little better.

I cut off a large chunk of leg and a small bit of stomach fat. For a moment, I considered killing my dinner. I quickly decided against it.

Death made the flesh taste gross.

I like to enjoy my meals.

I went upstairs to eat. If I wanted more, I'd head back to the basement for seconds.

In the kitchen, I sat at the table and began cutting the meat into bite-sized pieces.

The Accidental Murderer

I didn't have friends. So I had to entertain myself. Most days I ended up on the bridge, dropping rocks into the creek.

I liked making big splashes. So I found the biggest rock I could carry. And tossed it over the edge.

By the time I noticed the boat, it was too late.

The rock was already falling.

It bashed into the fisherman's head. It made a terrible sound.

He fell into the water. Blood bloomed on the surface, then slowly vanished.

The man didn't come back up.

Slowly, I realized what I'd done.

What I *was*.

A murderer.

What Death is Really Like

I run as fast as I can, but it's impossible to keep up. They've turned it up too high.

I stumble and fall. The speeding belt scraps my skin raw. Then I'm flying backward. I yell. I've fallen so many times already.

Every time he laughs at me.

"Get up!" the ghost says. He kicks me.

I groan.

He kicks harder.

"Up! You have to keep going!"

I sob as I'm shoved toward the treadmill. I get back on. I have to. Arguing makes it worse.

When I died, I never dreamed the afterlife would be nothing but endless exercise.

The Dangers of Dishes

I run as fast as I can, but it's impossible to keep up. They've turned it up too high.

I stumble and fall. The speeding belt scraps my skin raw. Then I'm flying backward. I yell. I've fallen so many times already.

Every time he laughs at me.

"Get up!" the ghost says. He kicks me.

I groan.

He kicks harder.

"Up! You have to keep going!"

I sob as I'm shoved toward the treadmill. I get back on. I have to. Arguing makes it worse.

When I died, I never dreamed the afterlife would be nothing but endless exercise.

Video Games

"Bye, Ron!" Mom called as she headed to work.

"Bye, Mom!" he replied.

All morning Ron focused on his game, enjoying the quiet. Mom was at work. His sister was at her friend's house for the weekend.

Around noon, Ron's stomach growled, demanding lunch. He paused his game and stood.

A hand closed around his wrist. Ron gasped. He thought he was alone.

A bloody girl appeared next to him. "Can I play next? I'm tired of watching."

"What?! No waay!"

"I want to play!" Her grip tightened.

"Help!"

But he was alone.

No one heard his yells become screams.

The Angry Spirit

The ghost never hurt anyone. Until the priest tried to banish it from its home.

Now it was angry.

Now it was dangerous.

It waited until the priest was gone. When everyone thought they were safe.

It waited until the family was sound asleep.

They thought the home was theirs now.

How very, very wrong you are, the ghost thought as it hovered over the sleeping parents.

It began to suck out the soul of the mother. Then, it did the same to the father.

They'd been safe until they brought the priest here.

They should have shared the home.

When the Power Goes Out

There's a storm raging outside.

I'm watching the weather channel when the power goes out.

I don't like it. It's too dark, too quiet.

I get up and stumble my way into the kitchen. I know I have some candles here somewhere.

Here! The candles! Now all I need is my lighter.

I get it lit and sigh with relief as a warm glow fills my kitchen.

"That's better," I mutter.

"No, it's not," someone whispers.

I go still.

I live alone.

"The dark is better," they rasp. A shadowy hand reaches over my shoulder and puts out the flame.

The Ghost in the Nursery

She watched the parents put their baby to sleep from the darkness of the closet. They kissed him goodnight and turned on the baby monitor before retreating to the living room. The little boy slept, oblivious to the danger he was in.

Soundlessly, she crawled from the closet, up the wall, and across the ceiling until she was directly above the crib. She stretched out a translucent arm. It stretched down into the child's mouth.

She tore out his soul, smiling as his heart and breathing stopped. Satisfied, she crawled back to the closet to wait for her next victim.

Silence

I hold the car door open for Terry. She's slumped and sad as she climbs into the car and sits in her booster seat.

"Daddy? Can we..." her question trails off as she sees my shaking head and dark expression.

My heart breaks as I buckle her in. I shut the door and go to the driver's side. I hate that I can't talk to my daughter.

Not one single word.

No "hello."

No "I love you."

I start the car as the ghost in the passenger seat smirks.

I hate the silence. But speaking would be far, far worse.

The Answered Prayer

Mommy and Daddy were fighting again.

I hid under the kitchen table with my eyes closed, crying as they battled. They used to love each other. Now all they did was fight.

I hated it. I wanted them to stop.

A friend told me about praying.

I decided to try it.

Please, God, make them stop!

POP!

The kitchen was silent.

I opened my eyes. Mommy and Daddy were gone. The room was coated in red gunk.

I closed my eyes again. *What did you do?!*

"I answered your prayer," a smug voice answered.

"G-God?"

"No. Not God. A ghost."

Calls From Rachel

Ring! Ring! Ring!

This was the tenth time today my phone had rung. Who the heck was calling me? Everyone knew I avoided actually talking to people on the phone like it was an infectious illness.

I'd rather die than call 911 for help. All my friends and family knew to text.

So who kept calling?

Ring! Ring!

Finally, I worked up all my courage and answered.

"Hello?"

"Jasmine… Help me. It's awful here," a voice rasped.

"Who…" I didn't finish. I was too shocked to finish.

"Rachel…."

I dropped the phone. That was impossible.

Rachel died five years ago.

The Laughing Baby

"Just get rid of it," her boyfriend said. "You can't have it! We aren't ready. It's not fair to us or the kid. You have to get rid of it!"

So she did.

It was gone.

It was over.

Until it came back to punish her.

Her aborted baby followed her everywhere now.

And only she could see it.

She gasped as it crawled across the ceiling, its black eyes hateful.

"Why'd you get rid of me, mommy?" it rasped.

A tear fell. "I'm so sorry."

"You will be."

It fell on her.

Her unborn baby laughed while she screamed.

The Ghost in the Corner

"I hate you!" she screamed at the top of her lungs. "You cheating bastard!"

"You're crazy!" he yelled back.

He was so confused. Just a second ago, he'd been fixing dinner. Then his wife came home and went nuts.

"I saw her! Just now! She was hugging you. Where'd she go?"

"What?!" They were alone "I'm calling the cops!"

"There! She's there! Get out, you bitch!" she screamed louded and started throwing plates at the corner of the room.

"Babe, there's no one there."

Then she thew the stew into the corner. And the house filled with screams of agony.

The Thing in the Attic

They hate me. I don't understand why. I'm not great, but I'm not nearly as bad as other ghosts.

I watch over the baby. I keep him safe at night.

They think I want to devour him.

They think it's scary when I rearrange the furniture. But I was just trying to make it nicer so they could enjoy it. They were terrified when I possessed Rich. I didn't want to hurt him.

I was trying to warn them.

If they hate me, what will they think of the thing hiding in their attic?

I hope they never find it.

The Forever Promise

He died in a car wreck. But he didn't know that.

No matter how many times I killed him, no matter what the method was, he kept coming back.

"Leave me alone," I begged as my son crawled into my shaking lap.

"But I love you, Daddy," he rasped. He rapped his cold, rotting arms around me.

"I l-love you too."

"I want to stay with you forever," he said.

"I know. But you're dead!"

"We promised we'd always be together!"

"I know!" I sobbed. "I remember!"

"So be happy, Daddy. I came back to help you keep your promise."

Deer Hunting

I followed my brother out of the woods.

He didn't know I was there. He thought I was dead. He shot me right in the face. He said he was in love with my wife. He said I was the only thing keeping them apart.

He invited me to go deer hunting with him.

Then.

He.

Shot.

Me!

What kind of brother did that!? Asshole!

It didn't matter that I was dead. He wasn't getting away with this.

I followed him home, growing angrier and angrier.

He.

Shot.

Me!

And I wasn't about to let him get away with it.

Possessed

We're drinking tea when it happens. At first, I thought I was imagining things.

Then the shadowy mass crawled inside my friend's ear. She shrieked and jumped up,

"Ah! There's something in my ear!"

"Shit! Are you okay?"

That was such a dumb thing for me to ask. Of course, she wasn't okay!

I just watched a creepy shadow thing crawl into her brain!

"Call someone!"

"Okay… who do I call?! Police?"

"An ambulance," my friend's lips moved. But it wasn't her voice.

I backed away. "What?"

"You're going to need one," she growled. Then she picked up a knife.

The Magnets

The first thing I did when I moved in was set up my fridge. I love magnets. My favorite where my cheesy letter-shaped ones for kids. I write swear words with them.

I finished and left to go unpack other things.

When I came back, I found the letter magnets rearranged.

Get out or die they now read.

"Holy shit!" I whispered.

I put them back the way I had them.

I left the kitchen, counted to 100, and went back.

Now they read *get out now.*

Maybe I should've listened when the realtor said my new house was haunted.

The Painting

"Do you like my painting?" May asked.

"It's not red enough," Kelly complained.

Mary frowned at her canvas. It was covered in dark red splotches. "Are you sure?"

"Very sure. It needs more red."

"But…" Mary tried to argue, but her protests faded when she saw how upset Kelly was.

Kelly's eyes had gone black, and the room was getting colder and colder.

"Redder!" Kelly demanded.

"Okay!" May held up her hands in defeat.

Kelly smiled demonically.

May looked at the dead body at her feet. If she wanted to keep Kelly happy, she was going to need more blood.

The Ghost's Cooking

Dirty dishes shattered around my feet. I couldn't believe this.

A bag of rat poison floated above the pot of stew I'd left simmering on the stove. Slowly, the bag opened and tipped over. Bright blue pellets splashed into the stew. A spoon floated up. It moved to the pot and stirred the poison in.

The foggy form of a woman appeared in front of the stove. She smiled. "Now you can finally kill your mother," she said before fading away again.

For a long moment, I just stood there, considering.

Then, I filled a bowl with the deadly soup.

Cold, Dead Kisses

I'm in bed. My limbs are rocks, pinning me to my mattress.

I know what's about to happen.

And I want to leave.

I want to *run*.

I try my hardest to move.

But I can't.

The door bedroom door opens and she comes to me. Just like she does every night.

She leans over me. She stinks of rot and death. Her lips are cold as she presses them against mine.

Her hair slaps me. It's wet, slimy, gross.

I sob as she crawls in bed with me.

I wish she'd stayed in the river where I left her.

The Frozen Hands

Mom makes us promise to stay in the backyard before she lets us play in the fresh snow.

We keep the promise.

For about an hour.

Then my brother starts a snowball fight. The fight takes us into the woods.

I start making a new snowball. Blue hand bursts from the snow and grab hold. I scream for my brother, but it's too late. More hands are rising from the snow.

Frozen hands pull me down into the cold.

"So cold."

"Join us."

"Company will keep us warm."

Snow fills my mouth as the frozen dead make me join them.

The Woods Will Claim You

She was so thirsty. And hungry. She'd been lost in the woods for two and a half days now. She was supposed to stay on the path. That's what mom said.

But she didn't.

Now she was in big trouble.

"Are you lost?"

"Hello?" she spun. She couldn't see anyone. "Who's there?"

"You're lost."

"Who's there!?" she demanded. She still couldn't see anyone.

"I've been watching you."

"I wanna go home!"

"You're not going home," the voice sounded sad.

"What? Why?"

"You're gonna die."

"I don't wanna!"

"Too bad. The woods will claim you tonight. Just like they claimed me."

The Email

The email was stupid.

It was just some dumb poem about death. Her cousin forwarded it to her. It claimed you had to send it to at least ten friends or you'd be cursed. If you didn't send it, you'd start seeing the dead.

And the dead would drive you mad.

It was stupid. What a waste of time. Curses weren't real!

She deleted it and went to bed.

Now, she wished she hadn't. Because she'd been wrong.

It *was* real.

So were the dead who kept whispering her name.

"Samantha…"

She wondered how long it took to go mad.

Wrong About Ghosts

A little girl has joined me on the park bench. She points at my book. "Whatcha reading?"

"A haunted house story," I said. I'm always happy to talk about books.

"Is it good?"

"So far."

"Is the ghost mean? Could it push people down the stairs and kill them?"

I sighed. Why did kids have to say such creepy things?

"No. In this book, the ghosts can't physically hurt people."

The girl looked disappointed. "They got it wrong."

"What do you me?"

"Ghosts can touch people. *Everyone* knows that."

I start protesting. But an invisible hand locks around my wrist.

The Thing Behind Him

He was home alone, watching TV when it happened. At first, he thought it was imagination. Or maybe a smudge on the screen.

But then it *moved*.

A dark, shadowy shape hovered in the doorway.

He tried ignoring it. *Just a shadow,* he thought stubbornly. He wasn't going to turn around. And he wasn't scared. Because *nothing* was there. *It'll go away soon.*

He managed to focus on the TV show for a few minutes. Then he glanced at the shadow.

It hadn't gone away.

It had come closer. Now it was right behind his chair.

Now he was scared.

The Face in the Mirror

The face I wear now isn't the face I was born with. That face is long forgotten, rotting away in a shallow grave in the backyard.

My wife killed me long ago. Back before the invention of TV and the other wonders of this modern world.

I don't mind this new face though. Sure, it might be a bit uglier than my original one, but this man's wife was much better than mine had been. Prettier too.

And now that I'd taken over his body, she was my wife.

I smiled.

I decided I liked the face in the mirror.

The Note and the Spiders

Mr. Green snatched the note from the two girls. They thought they were sneaky. They weren't.

"What do we have here?" he asked.

"Um…" Kelly said.

"Nothing!" said Jess.

Mr. Green unfolded the note and read it.

Did you bring them?

Yes. But I'm not sure I wanna do it.

You have to! The bullies will tell if you don't!

It'll be bad!

Everyone knowing will be worse!

"Don't do what?" Mr. Green demanded. He looked at Jess to find her opening a box she'd pulled from her backpack.

A box full of deadly spiders.

The room filled with screams.

The Swimming Pool

A smile took over my face as I watched my neighbor drive away. He was heading to his super boring office job.

What was I doing today?

I was heading to his backyard.

I couldn't believe I *just* realized I could borrow his pool while he was gone. *Was I dumb?* I wondered as I hurried outside.

Oh well. Better late than never.

"Whoo-hoo!" I cheered as I jumped into the deep end.

The water felt amazing.

Something brushed my leg. I opened my eyes. They stung, but that didn't matter.

All that mattered was the crocodile swimming toward me.

The Ants and the Kid

He'd had a terrible day at school. Why were his friends so mean?!

Could they even be called his friends if all they did was make fun of him and ruin his homework?

He stomped along the sidewalk, wishing for a way to take out his frustrations.

Then, halfway to his house, he saw it.

An anthill by a mailbox. They went about their little lives, oblivious to his bad day.

So he kicked it.

It felt good. He did it again.

It felt great.

Until the ants swarmed over him, stinging until he fell.

And didn't get back up.

Never Ever Leave

I'm never hungry. I'm never thirsty. Everything time I try, I throw it all up.

The doctors don't know what's wrong with me. They won't let me leave. I hate the hospital, its doctors, its nurses. Everyone keeps promising that they'll make me feel better.

But nothing is working.

Today, when a nurse tries to take my blood, nothing comes out.

"Huh," the nurse says. "That's weird."

I nod tiredly. "Yep," I agree.

I want to sleep. I can't do that either.

He leaves to go get the doctor.

While I'm alone, I cry.

Somehow, I know I'll never leave.

The New Chair

Grinning, I admired the new desk chair I'd gotten for my office. It was perfect. Practically brand new. I still couldn't believe I found it at a yard sale. What were the owners thinking, getting rid of this?

Still smiling, I sat down. It was so comfortable. I settled in to get some work done. I'd be so much more productive now.

My work went well.

For five minutes.

Then I felt itchy.

I looked away from my laptop to find my body covered with hundreds of spiders.

Deadly spiders.

I couldn't move to call for help. I was trapped.

The Oatmeal Nightmare

I yawned as I plopped down at the table. I watched a scary movie before bed. Needless to say, I was exhausted now. I wasn't looking forward to work.

"Good morning, sweetie," my husband said brightly and kissed me on the cheek. "How'd you sleep?"

"Terrible," I yawned. "What's for breakfast?"

"Oatmeal," he said and placed a bowl in front of me, along with my much-needed coffee.

I started eating but quickly realized something was wrong.

I looked closely at my bowl.

I screamed. The oatmeal was full of maggots.

This was the worst kind of nightmare.

The awake kind.

The Infestation

Frank thought the man was exaggerating when he said his basement was "literally full of snakes."

"It's completely full of snakes," the man warned Frank again as he led him to the basement.

"I think I can handle it."

"Are you sure?"

"I'm sure. This isn't my first rodeo," Frank promised.

He opened the door carefully. Just a quick peek to see what he was up against.

The room truly was full of withering, slithering, hissing bodies.

Slowly, Frank closed the door.

"See! literally full! Hey… you okay?"

Frank shook his head. "I think you need to call another exterminator."

The Bad Birthday Present

I wanted a dog for my birthday. I asked for one for months.

My parents got me an ant farm.

"You can start with these," Dad said. "If you do a good job with them, we'll see about getting you a dog next year."

I pretended to be happy.

I wasn't.

I was furious.

I waited until Mom and Dad were sleeping. Then I snuck into their room. I let the ants loose on their bed. The gross little bugs marched across the blankets towards my parents' faces.

Let them take care of the ants. Because I didn't want them.

The Cats

Molly rarely spoke to her neighbors and rarely left her apartment. So no one realized anything was wrong until the smell started to seep into the other apartments.

It was a bad smell. Rotting and gross.

So they called the police.

The police went to check on her. The apartment was dark, smelly, and full of at least twenty different cats. Skinny, hungry cats that tried to bite them as they entered the apartment.

They found Molly in the kitchen.

Well, they found her skeleton.

Turns out, the rumors that pets will eat their dead owners were very, very true.

Billy and the Bees

Billy sang along to his favorite song as he pulled up to his mailbox. The music was so loud, he didn't hear the angry buzzy that came from inside.

He opened the mailbox.

And unleashed hell.

Angry black and yellow hornets zoomed out of their metal prison and attacked the first thing they saw.

Billy.

He screamed and swatted wildly. It didn't do any good. It was one against hundreds. Maybe thousands. Billy screamed for help. He crawled from his car, trying to escape.

But the bees kept coming. They kept stinging.

Stinging.

Stinging.

Until Billy was still and silent.

II

91 Horror Drabbles

Book 2

The Monster Leaves the Basement

Melissa cowered in the corner of the kitchen, crying. Mommy went into the basement to get the Halloween decorations.

That was hours ago.

Melissa was sure the monster ate her. She *told* Mommy not to go down there! Why didn't she listen?!

Creak.

Melissa looked up.

Creak.

It was coming.

The door opened. A glowing face appeared in the shadows. The monster crawled toward her.

Melissa covered her mouth and closed her eyes, desperate to stay quiet. The monster hated noise.

"Boo!"

Melissa didn't move.

"You're quite… Good. You can live."

Melissa cried silently as the monster enjoyed her misery.

Inflight Meal

The airplane soars through a sea of white, puffy clouds. I can see people through the tiny windows. They look like they're either bored or asleep.

It's a normal, boring flight.

Until I swoop down and attack. I roar along with my stomach as I sink my claws into the metal. Along with the dying engines and the tearing of metal and flapping of my wings, I can hear the tiny screams of the helpless people inside the plane.

I rip off the roof and stick my head in. I snap up screaming humans, chew, and swallow. I love lunchtime.

The Skeletons Rise

The skeleton crawled out of the grave, pushing up through rocks and dirt. Its fingers dug into the muddy earth as rain pounded the graveyard. It moaned as it rose unsteadily to its feet. All around it, other skeletons rose up from their graves.

It turned and shuffled towards the entrance gates. The crowd followed. The skeleton led them out into the dark street. They had been put in the ground for years.

And they hadn't liked it.

Headlights came around the bend. The skeletons began to run. They swarmed the car. Thunder boomed, drowning out the passengers' terrified screams.

The Woman and the Mermaid

The woman walked along the beach listening to the small waves lapping at the sand. The moonlight shimmered on the water, and she was happy.

Then she heard it.

The singing.

That voice… it was… enchanting.

She scanned the beach, suddenly desperate to know the singer. It came from up ahead. She ran.

There!

Out in the water, atop a cluster of boulders, was a woman with a fish's tail instead of legs.

A mermaid.

She had to go to her. Without a second thought, she waded into the ocean, determined to meet the mermaid, forgetting that she couldn't swim.

The Hand Without a Body

The hand without a body wrapped its icy fingers around my ankle. I was too frightened to even scream as it yanked me from my bed. My pillows and blankets fell to the floor as I struggled.

I didn't want to go with it.

But it was strong.

Too strong.

I fell to the floor with a mighty *bang!*

The carpet burned as I was dragged from my room. I kicked and fought. I threw things at it.

But it didn't let me go. I only started screaming when I saw exactly where the hand was taking me.

The fireplace.

The Weeds

No matter how many times I pulled them up the weeds always came back.

Always.

Last night, I went to sleep proud of the work I did. But this morning I come outside to find them back and worse than ever.

No!

"Ugh! Damn it!" I grunt and swear, kicking at the bricks that surround my flowerbeds. I had them perfect yesterday. Now it looks like an overgrown lot no one's touched in three years.

Past my breaking point, I stomp to the shed to get the gas can. I grab a match too. I won't let the weeds win.

Zero Eyes and Three Heads

It had no eyes, this monster with three heads. It couldn't see me. But it still knew I was there, hiding and trembling just off the path.

I hunkered down, trying to make myself as small as possible. I didn't want to die. Not like this. Not as a monster's dinner.

I held my breath.

Maybe it wouldn't notice me. It couldn't see me. Not in the darkness. Not without eyes.

But it had dozens of ears.

It could hear me.

Slowly, one by one, its heads turned toward me.

I ran.

I was fast.

But the monster was faster.

The Tapping

Tap.

Tap.

Tap.

Something was at my window. It visited me every night.

I covered my ears. I didn't want to hear it.

The sound grew loud as it drummed its claws on the glass.

Tap!

Tap!

Tap!

I closed my eyes. I didn't want to see it either.

"Let me in…" It growled.

"N-never!"

TAP!

TAP!

TAP!

I worried my window would break. I didn't move. And finally, it left.

For now.

***

I lasted two more weeks.

Tap.

Tap.

Tap.
"Let me in…"
I couldn't take it anymore. Trembling, I opened my window.
And I let the monster in.

Watching the Beast

I did *not* want to watch this. But I couldn't look away.

My eyes were forced open. Straps kept me facing forward.

I *had* to watch as the beast cut into my husband's skull. He was awake, strapped to his own chair. He screamed. But he couldn't struggle.

I screamed too.

Blood and tears covered his terrified face. But the beast didn't stop. It *smiled*.

Once the skull was open, the beast got a bottle.

I gasped. "No!"

Acid.

The beast smiled wider. It opened the bottle.

It laughed at my distress.

And poured it right onto my husband's brain.

Monster Truck

Kevin slammed on the break, but it didn't do any good. The truck continued to zoom down the road at a hundred miles an hour.

He jerked on the wheel. The car still went straight down the highway. He tried changing the gear. No Luck.

He couldn't control his truck. He couldn't even escape. The doors stayed locked. His seatbelt stayed stuck.

What was going on?

What was he going to do?!

The radio turned on, and a growling voice said, "I'm in charge now."

"W-what… are you?"

"Monster Truck," it laughed.

"What do you want?"

"Kill!"

"Kill who?!"

"Everyone!"

Too Nice

My sister is nice today.

Too nice.

It's not normal.

I don't trust her. She's up to something. She must want something, so she's playing nice before asking for it.

I tiptoe to her room to spy on her. Maybe I'll overhear her call her friends, telling them about her plans.

Instead, I hear a gross, ripping sound.

Confusing and curious, I nudge her door open.

My sister's skin covers the bloody rug. In the middle of the gruesome mess stands a giant, lizard-like creature.

I scream. I *knew* it wasn't like her.

I *knew* she was too nice today.

Something's Still Inside Me

I gave birth to my baby this morning. It's a healthy baby girl. She's beautiful, healthy, and happy. I should be happy too.

But I'm not.

Because there's something still inside me.

I can feel it moving around in me.

Kicking.

Hitting.

Clawing.

I can feel talons scraping against the walls of my womb. It *hurts*. I try to tell the doctors and nurses. They don't believe me. They think I'm dramatic.

I'm not.

It kicks again. I can see the talons press against my stomach. It wants out. It's only a matter of time before its wish is granted.

How to Eat Humans

"Please! Don't eat me!" I sob, rattling the bars of my cage. "I don't taste good! People taste terrible!"

The giant glances up from his book to watch me curiously. He's wearing thick glasses and flipping through a book. If he wasn't forty feet tall and reading a book titled *How to Cook Humans,* he would've looked like a nerd.

"Well, *duh* you'll taste bad!" he laughs. He puts the book down next to my cage and goes to check the pot of water over his fire. "All meat does until you cook it! I have to boil you first."

New Neighbors and New Looks

She woke up to find her body melting. The bed was covered in blood and bits of soggy flesh.

"Damn it all!" she muttered and stumbled to the bathroom to check her reflection. Bits of her skull showed beneath the sagging, bloody mess of her liquefying skin.

She had worn this body for too long.

It was time for a new one.

Her feet left disgusting puddles as she went to peek out the window. She smiled when she saw her new neighbor coming outside to get the morning paper.

Val was pretty.

Val's skin would be perfect for her.

The Monsters in Our Jail

The guards think we are the monsters here. And yes, some of us are awful.

Murders.

Arsonists.

Rapists.

I'm a bank robber.

But us prisoners aren't the only monsters.

There are *things* here. Things that come out of the shadows late at night. Things that bite and claw and hurt.

I'm exhausted, but I can't sleep. I can hear one of the things outside my cell, scrapping its claws on the bars.

"I'm scared," my cellmate whispers.

I don't answer as the thing climbs onto my bed. I gasp in pain as teeth dig into my foot.

I'm scared too.

Kinks and Creeps

The guards think we are the monsters here. And yes, some of us are awful.

Murders.

Arsonists.

Rapists.

I'm a bank robber.

But us prisoners aren't the only monsters.

There are *things* here. Things that come out of the shadows late at night. Things that bite and claw and hurt.

I'm exhausted, but I can't sleep. I can hear one of the things outside my cell, scrapping its claws on the bars.

"I'm scared," my cellmate whispers.

I don't answer as the thing climbs onto my bed. I gasp in pain as teeth dig into my foot.

I'm scared too.

I wonder

Every night I check the locks on the doors and windows. Then I set the alarms. I make sure the surveillance cameras are working.

My house is secure.

But still, something gets in. It comes into my room. It stands over my bed and watches me sleep. I can't see it on the cameras. It's invisible.

But I can hear it.

I can *feel* it watching me.

I wonder how many eyes it has.

I know it has a big mouth. Every morning I find drool on me and my bed.

I wonder when it's going to eat me.

Just Like Alice

"You have to tiptoe here," I warned Jessica as we walked to the library.

"Why?"

"Because the monster hates kids who walk loud."

She laughed very meanly. "That's stupid! You're messing with me."

"No, it's true! That's what happened to Alice."

The news said she went missing. No one believed me when I told them what really happened.

She rolled her eyes. "I'm not falling for that!"

"Be careful!"

"Ugh! Whatever! You're such a baby!" She started walking past the house.

Stomp!

Stomp!

 Sto- "Ah!" she screamed.

I screamed too.

But it was too late. She was eaten.

Just.

Like.

Alice.

The Photo Monster

She hated taking pictures. There was something in the picture with her. A horrible strange thing that only she could see. A thing with tentacles, fangs, legs that were too long and too crooked.

And its eyes…

Its eyes were terrible.

Evil.

Hungry.

Wrong.

And every time her picture was taken, the thing crept closer to her.

It used to hide in the background, watching her from a long way away.

But now?

It was less than ten feet away. It could reach out and touch her if it wanted to.

She dreaded what would happen when it finally did.

The Big Book of Monsters

My son was so excited about his birthday present. I was proud I found such a cool gift.

A pop-up book featuring all kinds of monsters.

Vampires.

Werewolves.

Ghosts.

Trolls.

Every kind of monster. If you could imagine it, it was in there.

"Oh cool! Dad, look at this zombie- AH!"

I spun as his excited words turned into shrieks. I was just fast enough to see a green, rotting arm dragging my struggling child into the pages.

"Ralph!" I yelled. But I was too late.

He was gone.

Trapped in a book of monsters. A book I gave him.

The First Person

I took a deep breath before stepping out of the spaceship.

I did it! I was here!

I laughed giddily as I took another step.

I walked several dozen yards away from the ship, marveling at the alien landscape that surrounded me.

The radio in my spacesuit beeped. The other astronauts screamed.

"Hailey!"

"There's something behind you!"

I turned as the ground started shaking. "What?"

An alien monster the size of a house raced toward me. I screamed, ran, and tripped.

Fangs clamped around me.

The first person to walk on Mars.

And the first person to *die* on Mars.

They're Coming For Me

She creeps closer. It's impossible, but she does.

I killed her two weeks ago. I kidnapped her. I tortured her.

I *buried* her.

But now she's back.

Zombie! I realize in horror as she attacks.

She lumbers at me on broken legs. The one arm I left her is stretched out, her rotting fingers sticking out at odd angles. She moans low in her throat, almost a growl. I dodge around her and run for the backyard.

Once outside, I think I can get away.

Then I see them.

More of my victims hobbling from the trees.

Coming for me.

The Hands Made of Clouds

Everyone thought it was God at first. How could we not?

Giant hands made of clouds and light reached from the skies and picked people up.

It was amazing.

It was beautiful.

And those people?

They were delighted when they were picked.

We thought they were going to Heaven.

We thought God had finally returned to save us from this wretched world.

We were wrong.

The chosen ones began screaming.

Screams of pure terror. Of pure agony. We couldn't see them, but we knew.

Whatever was happening up there, it wasn't beautiful.

When the hands reached down again, we ran.

Whenever It Snows

I hate when it snows.

Snow means footprints. Footprints mean I can see the creature's path. How close it's coming to my house.

I don't know what it is. Its footprints don't look like any of the animals that live here. I checked. Whatever it was, it wasn't natural.

This morning, the snow is crisp and clean.

It's almost beautiful.

Except for the string of prints that comes and goes from the woods. Each print is as big as my stomach. They circle the house, getting closer and closer. Until they reach a big snowless spot outside my bedroom window.

The Thing in My Bed

The mattress dips as something joins me in bed.

Something *big*.

My stomach twists. My mouth goes dry. My heart beats way too fast.

But I don't move. I don't even open my eyes.

I'm too scared.

I live alone.

No kids.

No spouse.

No pets.

I lock my doors and windows. Nothing should be able to get in.

But it does. Every night it joins me, this thing.

I don't know what it is. But I know it's bad.

I'm not crazy. I know it's real. I can feel its stinking breath on my face.

I miss sleeping alone.

Rivers of Red

She hung by her intestines above our bed, swaying gently back and forth. Blood flowed down her body from horrible slashes across her throat, arms, and stomach. It made little red rivers down to her feet where it plopped rhythmically onto the bedspread.

Drip.

Drip.

Drip.

Went the blood.

Her eyes were wide and sightless, her expression still twisted in betrayed horror. She looked perfect like that. Smiling, I went to get my phone. I came back clearing my throat. Slowly, carefully, I punched the buttons.

Nine.

One.

One.

Time to sound scared.

Time for the performance of a lifetime.

The Weatherman

I hated him. He was fucking annoying. The weatherman. He was too perky.

Every.

Single.

Fucking.

Morning.

Every day my wife turned on the news, and there he was. Reporting temperatures and other shit I didn't care about.

I shuffled through the living room to the kitchen. I needed coffee before I pretended I didn't hate him. I opened the cabinet and got out the coffee can.

It was empty.

The weatherman droned on the TV. I couldn't take it. I grabbed a knife and keys. If my wife wouldn't stop watching him, I'd have to get rid of him.

The Razor

She slept sprawled across her bed, her covers kicked off. She looked comfortable.

I hated her for it.

I lay in my bed, watching her from across the dim room. I couldn't ignore the urge to hurt her anymore.

As quietly as I could, I crept from the room. I tiptoed to the bathroom and came back with a razor, one of the cheap pink disposable ones.

I placed it on her arm, just below the sleeve of her nightgown. I pressed the razor down. Hard. My sister's eyes fluttered open in confusion.

I jerked the razor.

My sister screamed.

Can't Say No

She peeked in on the baby around midnight. He was asleep in his crib. Gently, she shut the door again and tiptoed to her daughter's room. The four-year-old sucked her thumb in her sleep. Her other arm clutched a plush alligator.

She smiled sadly before closing the door and going to the kitchen. She turned on all the burners and started a fire.

Then she got in her car and drove away. She cried the whole time, but she didn't stop. God wanted her babies back. He told her so in her dreams.

And she couldn't say no to God.

Leah's Treasure's

At recess, my friends show off their treasure chests. Boxes full of jewelry, pretty rocks, and toys.

"Leah! Did you bring yours?" Ally asks.

"Yeah…"

"Let us see!"

Everyone nods.

I hesitate. I don't have jewelry or toys.

Will they laugh?

"Please!?" Astrid begs.

I pull the shoebox from my backpack. I open it, desperate for their approval.

I don't get it.

My friends run screaming when they see what's inside. Sadly, I look down at my beloved collection of human fingers. I didn't understand. Where my treasures really that scary?

I go to ask the teacher what she thinks.

The Stolen Cake

I couldn't believe it. My roommate was the absolute worst! She stole my last piece of cake. I was saving that! And she stole it! She was *such* a selfish jerk.

I wasn't going to let her get away with this.

I was going to get revenge.

All evening I acted like nothing was wrong. Like I wasn't pissed off beyond belief. I pretended I was fine.

Then, once she went to bed, I acted. I snuck into the kitchen and mixed laxatives into her jug of tea.

Ha!

That would teach that bitch not to mess with my sweets.

Ears and Knives

He cried as he studied himself in the mirror. He hated himself. He was ugly. His ears were the worst part. They were so big and gross.

They had to go.

He looked down at the counter. On it, sat a towel and a knife. He picked up the knife and placed it against the top of his ear, right next to his skull.

One.

Two.

Three.

He started to cut. It hurt so bad. But he kept cutting.

Blood was everywhere. On his arms, on the counter. He felt sick.

But happy.

He moved on to his other ear.

The Man With the Chainsaw

The man loomed over me, laughing crazily. But his laughter was lost beneath the roar of the chainsaw.

I screamed, begging for my life. "Don't do it! Please don't do it! Please! Just let me go!" I wanted to run, but chains on my neck and wrists trapped me in the corner of the bloody, disgusting shed.

The chainsaw stopped, and the shed slowly filled with silence. The man tilted his head to the side, considering.

"Let you go?"

"Yes! Please! I won't tell anyone!"

He thought some more. He shook his head.

Laughing, he turned the chainsaw back on.

Sick

I feel terrible. I can't get out of bed. I'm hot. I'm dizzy. My head feels like it might explode. My stomach feels like last night's dinner is boiling inside me.

I know I'm going to throw up, but I'm too weak to get to the bathroom. It takes all my strength just to scoot to the edge of the bed.

"Oh, God," I mumbled. My stomach heaves. Burning gunk shoots up my throat and out of my mouth as I start to vomit.

Ugh.

When I'm done, I glare at the pile of half-digested organs. Cannibalism isn't for me.

In the Car With a Mad Man

The car zooms too fast around the bend. I slam into the door, grunting in pain. Police serins wail behind us.

the man in the driver's seat ignores me. His hands are white on the steering wheel. His eyes look too big for his face. He's insane, I'm sure.

And I'm trapped with him.

How did my day go so wrong? I just ran out to the store for coffee. Now I've been carjacked by a man with a gun.

"Where are we going?" I sob.

"Hell," he says. Then he jerks the car off the side of the cliff.

The Wicked Stepdaughter

"I hate you! You're the worst!"

"Don't be so dramatic."

"I do! I hate you! And your stupid family!"

"They're your family now too."

"Dad married you! Not me! You're not my real family!"

I rub my temples. My stepdaughter is giving me a headache. All this arguing because I asked her to clean up the living room?

"Please, I don't want to argue. Can't you-"

"No! Screw you! Do it yourself!"

"Sky-"

"Leave me alone!"

"Or what?" I demand, losing my patience.

"I'll kill you!"

I want to call bullshit.

But that look in her eyes...

She means it.

What We Did Last Night

My wife, daughter, and I sit together in church. The sermon is about to start. I glance at my family. My wife chats with her friend. My daughter stares at her phone. She's upset. Her boyfriend hasn't texted her good morning.

"Relax, Sweetie. Ryan's probably sleeping."

She shakes her head. "What if something's wrong?"

I shift uncomfortably. I can feel God watching me.

He knows I'm lying.

He knows we've broken one of the Ten Commandments.

We *murdered* Ryan. We bashed his skull in and buried him in the woods.

Now we're pretending everything is fine.

I'm going to Hell.

The Celebrity and the Mob

"Oh my god!"

"It's him!"

They scream and rush at me. I try to duck away, but there are too many people. They surround me. They yell and squeal. People demand my autograph. A man twice my age begs me to marry him. A woman hugs me. Someone pulls my arm. It *hurts*.

I can barely breathe. I'm trapped.

I'm frightened enough to yell, "Stop! Let me go!"

They don't like that. Their excitement becomes anger.

They pull harder, scream louder. They're crazy. My hair is yanked out, my arm twisted.

They're going to kill me.

I can't stop them.

Crushing My Coworker

He screamed for help. He swore he'd do whatever I wanted if I would *please* turn it off.

I laughed and told him no, even though I knew he couldn't hear me over the whirl of the machine and his own screams.

I hated him.

He deserved this, the pretentious prick. I had worked here *way* longer than him. I didn't need him telling me how to use the cardboard baler.

The screaming stopped. Red goo seeped from the bottom of the machine.

Still laughing, I went to open the door and admire the crushed mess of my former coworker.

She'll Always Find Me

I sit on the bed and look around the tiny one-room cabin. I'm in the middle of nowhere, alone in the woods far, far away from civilization.

No running water.

No internet.

No electric.

I told no one where I was going. I'm completely alone.

I should feel safe here. I don't. I'm terrified.

Because today in the day. She's getting out of prison today. And I know she'll come for me.

She won't kill me. That'd be too kind.

I know deep down, running is pointless. Even way out here, I know she'll find me.

She always finds me.

The Peaceful Dinner

I smiled as I spread my fanciest cloth napkin across my lap. Everything was ready.

Candlelight. Classic music playing in the background. Organic, expensive food. The fanciest wine. I had to save up forever to buy it all. It was worth it.

Especially when I got to enjoy it alone.

Yes, I thought as I surveyed my setup. *It's perfect.*

Especially my cup and silverware. Those, I was most proud of.

The fork, knife, spoon?

Carved from my wife's bones.

My wine glass?

My infant daughter's skull.

This was the only way I could enjoy my perfect dinner in peace.

The Screaming Game

She hadn't made a sound.

Yet.

He was impressed. Usually, his playmates screamed by now. They cursed him too.

Not her.

She just cried silently, the tears making rivers down her bloody cheeks.

He'd taken all of her toes, three fingers, her right ear, and removed the skin on her left arm. Watching her muscles twitch… it was fascinating.

What should he take next?

What would hurt the most?

He had to make her scream before midnight. If he didn't, he had to let her go. He couldn't let that happen. This was his favorite game. And he hated losing.

Budgeting

I threw the calculator across the kitchen, growling in frustration. It didn't matter how many pennies I saved, or how many extra shifts I took. We were always broke, always behind, always in debt.

No food.

No money.

No lights if I didn't pay the bill by Friday.

What was I going to do?

I was so tired.

So stressed.

So scared.

Crying, I looked over my mess of bills and mail.

Then I saw it:

My wife's life insurance policy. If she died in an "accident" I'd have plenty to take care of the kids.

The budget was saved.

Snuff Film

She looked so pretty tied to the bed. So scared and small and helpless. Her eyes were big and pleading as I checked the ropes one last time. The knots were perfect. No way she could get loose and ruin the video.

"There," I said and patted her on the head. "Ready!"

She tried to scream something, but it was muffled by her gag.

"Don't be that way," I chuckled as I went to get the camera and knife. "This is your fault. You wanted to be a movie star. You should've been more specific about what *kind* of film."

Force Feeding

"No more!" I cried, throw-up dripping down my chin. I literally couldn't eat anymore. Everything the woman forced down my throat came right back up.

"Yes more!" she snapped and smashed a lump of chocolate against my mouth. "Eat it! Eat it now!"

"No!"

"Yes!"

"I can't!" I sobbed.

"Eat it! Or your brother goes back in the oven!"

I glanced at my brother. Just the word over made him shake with terror. He was already so burned and bloodied. He wouldn't survive another time out in the oven.

Cringing, I opened my mouth and took another bite of candy.

Vacation

The kids pounded on the basement door. I ignored them as I tripled checked the locks that would keep them safe for the next two weeks.

"Mommy! Let us out!"

"Don't leave!"

I shook my head and went to get my bags. I had a flight to catch.

The kids would be fine down there while I was gone. There was a bathroom, a bed, plenty of food and drinks. I even put the TV down there, so they'd have entrainment while I was gone.

I'm not a monster, I assured myself.

I was tired.

And I *needed* this vacation.

The Tenth Time

The first time I killed someone, I didn't want to. I was desperate. I needed the money.

The second time, it was an accident. I just wanted her to stop crying.

The third time I killed someone, it was self-defense. I just couldn't work with that bitch anymore. I did it to save my sanity.

The fifth time I killed, it was for profit. I needed my inheritance.

The sixth time, I killed for kindness. Grandma missed Grandpa so much. She wanted to see him again.

By the tenth time, I stopped making excuses.

I admit it.

I like killing.

Thunderstorm

The sound of glass shattering wakes me.

For several moments, I lie there, tired and confused. What's happening?

Then I hear her scream.

I bolt up. "Annie!" I shriek and run to her room.

I fling the door open. My heart pounds in my throat.

The bedroom is empty.

My baby is gone.

The window is broken, the curtains ripped down.

I rush to it, squinting into the darkness. Glass digs into my bare feet. Blood mixes with mud, rainwater, and toys on the fairytale-themed rug.

I scream my daughter's name.

There is no answer.

Just the boom of thunder.

Spring Cleaning

I found it while cleaning out the basement, a boring and dirty chore my wife forced on me every spring. She knew how much I hated the cold and the dark and the spiders.

But this year?

The cleaning was worth it.

Because I found it.

My late Father-in-Law's gun. My wife hated guns and tossed it down here months ago, refusing to have anything to do with it.

I smiled and pointed it. It felt so nice in my hands.

The gun.

My way out of a hellish marriage.

Back to cleaning.

All I needed now were the bullets.

The Priest

"Heaven needs angels! It needs warriors! Every soul we can send it to help in the war against Satan helps." The priest spoke passionately as he wandered the pews, making sure all the children drank.

He paused to smile encouragingly at a mother in the front row.

She cried silent tears as she urged her son to drink the rest of his kool-aid.

The priest tilted the toddler's sippy cup so he could finish the last drops. "He'll be a fine addition to God's army," he promised the mother.

The mother forced a smile and dried her tears. "I'm proud."

Watch Out For the Ghosts

WATCH OUT FOR THE GHOSTS!

I scoffed at the sign in the apartment complex's laundry room. It was written in all capitals with glitter paint on pink poster board.

I chuckled to myself and picked a washing machine.

Ghosts? Seriously?

Ha!

It was obviously someone's attempt at a joke.

A poor one.

I opened the washer to dump my clothes in.

Inside the washer, a bruised and beaten baby floated face down in bloody water. I slammed the lid and scurried back, trembling.

When I worked up the courage to look again, it was empty.

Guess the sign was serious.

Trapped in the Trunk

It's cold.

It's dark.

But I can't leave.

A long, long time ago my friend put me in her. She bashed me over the head and strangled me. Then she stuffed me a trunk and buried it beneath the basement.

I died that day. But I didn't go to Heaven. I stayed with my body.

I beat against the trunk's lid, but no one comes.

Maybe they can't hear me?

Maybe they don't care.

Thump.

Thump.

Thump.

I smack the walls of my too little prison. If I ever get out of here, I'm going to destroy my so-called friend.

Words I Didn't Write

I was on a roll. But it was about to be ruined.

Stupid nature!

How dare my body need to go to the bathroom in the middle of my writing time. My book was *way* more important than going pee.

I swore and pushed away from my desk. I hurried to the bathroom, muttering bits of dialogue to myself.

I ran back to my office when I finished. I placed my hands on the keyboard.

I froze.

There were more words on the screen than before. Words I didn't write.

I love watching you write.

Keep writing, Mel.

Or else.

Brittney and the Board

I don't want to play. Mama says Oujia Boards are evil.

But all my friends want to. I can't be boring. So I put my finger on the pointer alongside my friends'.

Brittney goes first. Prissily she asks, "Are there spirits here?"

Nothing happens.

"Maybe the ghosts don't like you," Cassidy giggles.

"Oh, hush!" Brittney pushes the game away.

I sigh, relieved.

"Let's do something else," Brittney grumbles.

"Hey! Do you think Brittney's a jerk?" Miranda asks. "Is that why you wouldn't answer?"

Brittney squeaks, gesturing at the board.

The pointer moves. But no one's touching it.

Moves towards "yes."

The Blood Man

I keep a bookshelf in front of my closet. My girlfriend thinks I'm nuts.

"Why are you scared?" she asks constantly. "You're not five! Don't be a baby!"

I wish I was five. It's cute when five-year-olds are scared of monsters in the closet.

When adults do it, it's stupid and immature.

My girlfriend doesn't understand. She can't see or hear the bloody, soulless, dead man who lives in my closet. If she ever saw him, I know she'd be terrified too.

He wants out.

That's why the door is blocked. It's the only way to keep my girlfriend safe.

This is My House

I watch them from the darkness under the porch as they approach my house.

It's old and falling apart, but it's *mine*.

I won't let anyone take it away.

There are three invaders.

A vampire.

A princess.

A superhero.

They carry glowsticks and buckets of goodies. They look cute, but I don't care. They're trespassing.

The princess steps on the porch.

I attack.

I fly out of the darkness. My eyes glow, teeth bared. The princess screams as I drag her into the dark. Her friends run and scream.

I'm proud. This is my house.

And I must protect it.

The Laughing Ghost

She stumbled and fell to the ground, sobbing. She had to get away. It was going to kill her if she didn't. She could hear it behind her, getting closer and closer. It's terrible, manic, otherworldly laughter echoed off the trees.

"Leave me alone!" she croaked as she forced herself back to her feet.

The laughter continued.

Louder.

Closer.

She started running again and almost imminently slammed into a tree. She swore and kept going. It was so dark, so cold. She didn't want to die, but how could she escape a ghost?

Eventually, she'd need rest.

Not a ghost.

Forever and Ever

I float next to my body, surrounded by cold, dark water and the occasional disinterested fish. I used to love the lake. It was once my happy place.

Now it's my prison.

Forever.

My body is nothing but bones now. Cold, dead bones stripped of all its flesh by the fish who now ignore me.

I kind of miss the fish.

Is that weird?

High above me, on the sunny surface of the lake, a boat full of laughing, happing people float by. I hate myself for it, but I wished one would fall in, drown, and join me.

Forever.

How to Help a Ghost

Help Me.

The words were on the bathroom mirror.

I should've run. Instead, I whispered, "How?"

The words changed.

Let Me Out.

"Out?"

The Sink.

"What?" It was all I could think to say.

Look Down The Drain.

I didn't want to. But my feet had a mind of their own. I stumbled forward, fell against the vanity.

I looked. I gasped.

An eye blinked at me.

"What are you?!"

The words on the mirror changed.

Ghost.

"Oh… How do I help?"

Feed Me.

"Feed you?"

Blood.

I didn't want to. But I couldn't stop.

I reached for my razor.

The Man in the Attic

He's trapped in my attic, the man I killed. Not his body, thank God. That'd be disgusting. I buried him in the desert. No one would ever find him.

No body, but his soul is still trapped up there. He's loud and annoying, always stomping about and banging on the pipes.

Maybe I shouldn't have killed him. But he deserved it. He was trespassing. I was only defending myself.

Thump!

I put a pillow over my head. He hadn't let me sleep since I killed him.

Would I ever sleep again?

As if to answer my question, he started screaming.

The Goodest Ghost

I wait by the gravestone every day, hoping my best friend will come back.

I miss her.

I want to play fetch again. I want my ears scratched. I want to sit beside her and watch TV. She always laughed when I barked at the doorbells.

But more than anything, I want to hear her voice. Hear her say, "Who's a good boy?"

Snow begins to fall. Determined to wait, I lay down.

So cold.

I close my eyes.

When I wake up, her arms are around me. I'm warm again.

"Who's a good boy?" she sobs happily. "You are."

My Only Friend

I struggled on the bed, but straps held me in place. All around stood my parents, the priest, and the paranormal investigators. They hated my friend. They wanted to take her away.

They said they wanted to help. I didn't think it was helpful at all.

I sobbed as the priest opened his Bible and began reciting prayers. He sprinkled me with holy water.

It burned.

My friend screamed in pain and rage as she was forced out, rising from my body in a cloud of smoke and shadows.

I screamed too.

My only friend was gone.

I was alone.

The Lonely Little Shadow

My phone rings. Annoyed that my TV show was interrupted, I answer it.

"I'm in your basement..." A voice says. "Can I come up? I'm so lonely..."

I hang up. *Prank. Just ignore it.*

I manage it for an hour.

Then there's a knock at my door. I freeze. It's midnight. I'm home alone.

"Lemme in! I'm lonely..." It's the voice from the call.

I get up to lock the door.

It's too late.

The door's already opening.

A shadow without a body crawls toward me.

And into my bed.

"So... Lonely..." it whispers. "Can I stay?"

Terrified, I nodded.

The Ghost in the Grave

She pounded frantically on the lid of her coffin. She screamed. She howled. She begged.

But no one heard her.

Because no one came to visit her.

She twisted, trying to get comfortable. It was impossible. Especially with her rotting body taking up so much of the cramped, wooded prison.

She hated this. She'd been trapped in here so long. Years and years and years. She should have told them to cremate her when she had the chance. Now she was stuck here in her own grave with her own, stinking maggot-infested body.

Death was just as bad as life.

Someday You'll Be Free

I waited until the mom and dad were asleep in their room before creeping out of the darkness of the closet. The child sobbed silently, clutching a ragged doll. Bruises and blood covered her body. She'd been punished for "stealing" food.

I hated her parents.

I wanted to save her.

I wasn't strong enough.

Yet.

But I would be.

Someday.

I crawled across the wall and onto the child's bed. I crouched next to her, stroking her hair comfortingly. Slowly, she stilled and slept.

"I'll save you," I promised. "Someday, they'll be dead too. Like me. Then you'll be free."

So I did and So I Will

My afterlife started with a game of truth or dare.

My friends dared me to ring Mr. Freeman's doorbell and run away.

So I did.

They dared me to break into the library and spray paint the walls.

So I did.

They dared me to kill all the horses on Ms. Brown's ranch.

So I did.

I thought they'd dare me to kill a person next.

Nope.

They dared me to jump off the tallest building in town.

So I did.

Now I'm a ghost.

My new friends dared me to haunt and kill my old ones.

So I will.

The Baby's Cries

Late at night, always after midnight, the crying starts. The sound of a baby.

The sounds of my sweet grandchild.

Cold.

Terrified.

Alone.

I hate that he's suffering. But there's nothing I can do for him.

Not now.

Not when he's already dead.

I don't blame my daughter. She didn't know what she was doing. She's sick, her brain sad and broken.

I blame myself. I should have known better than to leave her alone with him.

Downstairs, the baby begins crying. The horrible sound comes from where my daughter put him down for his very last nap.

The fridge.

What does the Cat See?

"Aw! Look how cute he is, staring at the wall," Mommy laughs.

"What do you think cats see when they do that?" Daddy asks.

"I don't know. Is there a bug?"

"I don't see one," Daddy picks me up. "Come here, kitty bean. Whatcha looking at?"

I can't answer.

They don't speak cat.

Daddy holds me and scratches my cheek how I like. Pets and cuddles usually make me happy.

Not today.

Not with the soulless thing watching us. The thing only I can see.

I hiss.

It laughs.

"There's nothing there, silly," Mommy says.

She doesn't know she's lying.

The Ghost Who Loved to Cook

The ghost slipped into the mind of the sleeping mother and took over her body. She struggled for a moment before he lulled her back to sleep.

Happy, he took her body to the kitchen. It took a bit to get used to it.

Once he was used to controlling her, he started cooking. He made gravy. Chopped vegetables. He prepared sauce.

Oh, damn it.

He needed meat to complete his dish.

He checked the fridge, but there wasn't any in there. *That's okay,* he thought. He took a knife to the daughter's bedroom. He knew where to find some.

Taking Her Toy Away

Have you ever had to take a toy away from your child?

I have.

It wasn't punishment. It was protection.

My daughter has a favorite doll. A lovely old cloth doll. I had to take it from her. She begged for it back.

It broke my heart. But I couldn't give in.

That doll was dangerous.

It moved on its own.

It whispered things to me.

Awful things.

Taking it away was the best way to keep her safe.

I just hope the doll can't dig its way out of its grave.

Or find its way out of the woods.

The Bus Driver

The driver hated her job. She hated being scared. But she couldn't afford to leave it, no matter how much she wanted to tell her boss to fuck off.

As she drove her regular route, she occasionally glanced at the passengers in the mirror. There were the normal boring faces of tired people, eager to get home after a long day.

Then there were the dead people.

The shadowy ones with red eyes. The grey, transparent ones with bloodstains and sinister expressions.

She didn't know what they wanted. Only that they moved closer to the front with every bus ride.

The Queen's Nightmare

"Captain! Bring forth the condemned!" Queen Annabell demanded.

Reluctantly, I obeyed, dragging the prisoner into the center of the throne room.

"I'm sorry," I muttered and pushed him to his knees.

The man only refused to bow. If it were up to me, I'd flog him and send him on his way.

But the Queen wanted to make an example of him.

So he had to die.

"This is what happens to those who refuse to respect the crown!" she yelled to the crowd.

I rushed backward as the nightmare shadow creatures slithered from the darkness to devour the man.

The Jar of Ghosts

The witch smiled at her new apprentice as she showed off her collection of trapped souls. The dead she used in her darkest spells. The foggy grey masses of energy swirled around their prisons.

They whispered angrily, swearing vengeance on the witch who trapped them. Too bad they couldn't open jars from the inside.

"Wow," the apprentice whispered in amazement as she took in the basement filled with thousands of jars. "These are all ghosts?" She picked one up for a closer look.

"Yes. Be careful. Don't-"

The jar slipped.

Crash!

"Drop that," the witch groaned as the ghost escaped.

The Haunted Hotel

Cops swarm the hotel, desperate to find the child. The parents cry as a cop questions them. Another cop checks the security footage. More question the guests and staff.

This isn't the first child to vanish here.

She won't be the last.

Across the hall, a door creaks open on its own. Two shadows slip out of a room. One is crooked and bent, too tall to be human. The other is the trembling outline of a girl.

The tall one turns to glare at me. It raises a finger and beckons me. Terrified but unable to disobey, I follow.

Joining the Ghost

I place the gun to my temple, smiling. My family members are all around me. I shouldn't be able to see them, but I can.

Great Aunt Matilda, who died in her sleep.

Grandpa Mason, who died of cancer.

Cousins Ruth and Ester. They died in a car accident.

There are so many others. I miss them. I want to hug them.

But I can't. The living can't hug the dead. But if I join them…

I take my last breath…

And pull.

BANG!

I open my eyes and smile widely as the loving arms of the dead surround me.

A Bad Day at the Petting Zoo

It was such a beautiful spring day. Nice and sunny. It'd be a shame to waste it. So I got my daughter, and off to the zoo we went. After seeing her favorite wild animals we wound up in the petting zoo.

"I'm gonna pet them all!" she cheered, skipping into the pen holding goats, sheep, and miniature horses.

I sat on a bench to check my texts.

"Mommy! Look!"

I did. My phone fell and shattered on the sidewalk.

My daughter was holding a snake. A *poisonous* snake.

I screamed. But it was too late.

The snake bit her.

Hidden in the Car

The car salesman seems nervous as we buckle up. He's sweating slightly and sits stiffly in the passenger seat.

He's young, so I decide he must be a new hire. *He's just nervous,* I tell myself.

I want him to relax. I comment on the nice weather, trying to put him at ease.

It's not working.

I admire the car's interior. I open the glove compartment.

"Don't!"

"Why?"

"Those!"

I jerk back. Inside the glove compartment is a nest of hornets. The mean kind you see on TV. I guess this explained why such a nice car was so cheap.

Trapped in a Tree

Hallie's shoulders shook as she clung to her tree. She still couldn't believe she'd been so stupid. She should've known better, should've known it was a trick. Why would the popular kids want to hang out with a loser like her?

They invited Hallie on a hike. And she stupidly said yes.

Now she was stuck in a tree. Laughing, they dared her to climb it. Then they left her there.

She hugged the tree, too scared to get down on her own.

Her branch shook, and she looked up. A buzzard had landed next to her. Hallie sobbed harder.

The Kitchen at Midnight

Her stomach growled loudly. Guess she hadn't eaten enough for dinner. She yawned and got up. She'd have a quick sandwich then go back to bed.

She made her way to the kitchen. It was slow going. She'd just moved to this new house, and she was still getting used to the new layout. She got lost last night trying to find the bathroom.

She fumbled for the switch. Ha! There it was.

Click!

The kitchen flooded with light. Her screams echoed off the walls and hundreds, no *thousands,* of roaches ran for the walls, trying to escape the light.

Seeing Dinosaurs

"This is your third wish," the genie said. "You must use it wisely."

I thought hard. I

wished to be the richest man in the world.

Then I wished to be able to breathe underwater. I always want to do that.

I decided to wish for something money couldn't buy.

"I wish to see dinosaurs."

The genie snapped his fingers. We were in a jungle.

The ground started shaking.

Boom.

Boom.

Boom.

As the T-rex came closer I realized I'd made a mistake. I should've wished to see dinosaurs *safely*.

"Have fun!" the genie said before vanishing.

The T-rex roared.

Fluffy is Friendly

"Do you want to come up?" my friend asked. "You can meet Fluffy."

"Fluffy?"

"Yeah, she's my kitty."

I nodded. As we climbed the stairs to her tenth-floor apartment, I pictured a little white kitten in a feathery bed.

"Here we are!" She unlocked the door.

We stepped inside.

The first thing I noticed was the smell. Like rotting meat and shit. Then I saw the claw marks on the walls.

"Fluffy!"

The floor shook as a tiger emerged from the bedroom.

"Don't worry. Fluffy's friendly." she insisted.

I screamed as the animal charged at me.

"She'll kill you quickly."

The Things I told Myself

I didn't think my husband was serious when he said he'd push me off the cruise ship.

He wasn't.

I told myself the ship would come back for me.

It didn't.

I told myself I would be found quickly.

I wasn't.

I told myself the dark shapes in the water were dolphins. Smart, friendly dolphins that would help me get to shore.

They weren't.

I told myself the sharks weren't hungry.

They were.

I was desperate. Scared. I told the sharks to leave. I begged them to go away.

They didn't.

I told myself things would get better.

They didn't.

Snakes in the Park

He cried as his pets vanished into the small wooded area of the park. Those were his babies.

But they were too big. He couldn't afford to keep feeding them all.

Plus, his neighbors were starting to ask questions. He wasn't supposed to have pets. He couldn't afford to lose his apartment.

So he had to let them go.

He had to say goodbye.

He hoped they would be happy here. He hoped they would have enough to eat.

But mostly, he hoped no one saw them and freaked out about the hundreds of poisonous snakes in the city park.

The Grossest Game Show

The game was simple.

Eat gross things for money.

The longer the game went on, the grosser the foods became. If you refused, you lost all your money.

So far Sandra had eaten raw eggs, stewed rat brains, and even raw squid.

Time for the next challenge.

A covered plate was placed in front of her. The lid lifted, revealing…

Live maggots and ants wiggled in a bowl.

Sandra cringed as she picked up her spoon. She scooped up the bugs. She shoved them in her mouth and began chewing. Disgusting! But she refused to lose.

She swallowed another bite.

The Crawling Spider

The spider was deadly.

But really? How dangerous was a little spider? One good swat would kill it.

Of course, that only worked when the person could move.

And Brent's sister was tied to the bed. She couldn't do anything but tremble as the spider crawled up her body.

Tears leaked from her eyes as Brent poked and prodded it, making it mad. She was gagged, but she still tried to beg. Brent ignored her, grinning wickedly as the spider crawled to her face.

The grin widened as it bit her tear-filled eye.

That'd teach her to steal his allowance.

Polly Wants

"Fuck you, bitch!" Polly told me one morning.

I brushed it off, figuring it was the kids. What teen *wouldn't* want a swearing parrot?

Then Polly started saying really disturbing things.

"Polly wants to eat you!" Polly said whenever I passed her cage.

The kids swore they didn't teach her that one.

"Polly watches you sleep," she said before I went to bed one night.

"Whatever," I huffed, annoyed.

I woke up in the middle of the night. Polly stood on my dresser, watching me with red, glowing eyes.

"Polly?" I whispered.

"Polly is going to kill you!" she cawed.

Feeding the Pigs

The pigs squealed with excitement as Jeff approached their pen. They jostled each other, fighting for the best spot at the trough.

"Who wants breakfast?" Jeff smiled as he dumped his bucket of intestines over the fence. The guts smacked against the rusty metal, old blood, and bits of guts splattering everywhere.

The pigs attacked the food like they were starving. That couldn't be further from the truth.

Jeff's smile grew wider as his pigs ate. It was hard finding new victims to feed them. But it made the bacon taste so good that it was worth the extra effort.

The Hungry Crow

I cried as they pushed me into the tall, skinny cage. The door slammed closed. I was trapped.

No way out.

No way to even sit down.

I begged for mercy. But no one listened to me. I was a murderer, they said. I deserved to suffer.

"Please! I didn't do it!"

My cage was raised to the top of the city walls. So everyone could watch my punishment.

Another cage swayed in the breeze beside me. The person inside was long dead, their face eaten by birds.

A crow landed on the bars of my cage, cawing loudly.

Hungerly.

They're Following Me

They're always following me, always watching. I think they're waiting for something.

But I'm not sure what.

My boyfriend thinks I'm being paranoid.

I'm not.

I *know* the rats are following me.

I pointed one out on our walk home today. "There!"

"Babe," he sighs. "We're in New York! It's full of rats. Just ignore them."

I try to.

But it's hard when I can see their beady eyes watching me from every alley, every storm drain.

"Maybe they want to eat me," I whisper.

"Don't be ridiculous!"

He laughs.

I don't.

One of the rats is creeping towards me.

In the Snake Enclosure

The snake wrapped around me, crushing me. I tried to scream, but all my air was gone. The snake squeezed tighter. My vision went dark from the pain. I felt my ribs crack, then break.

I was going to be eaten, I realized with dawning horror. This was the end. I would die here, trapped in a snake enclosure at a zoo no one even came to anymore.

The snake moved, adding even more pressure. I felt like I was fading away. I couldn't even cry.

Fangs dug into either side of my head as it started to swallow me.

Slugs and Bugs

Grandma and Grandpa won't let me leave the dinner table until I eat everything.

I'm so hungry. I haven't eaten since breakfast yesterday.

But this meal we're having…

I don't want this.

The bowl is filled with slimy slugs, crawling ants, and wiggling worms. Watching the creatures moving around, trying to escape my bowl makes me want to throw up. I look at my family members. My siblings and grandparents eat happily.

My brother slurps a worm like it's a noodle. "Try 'em, Sis!"

I gag but reach for my fork. I don't have a choice. It's bugs or nothing.

III

101 Horror Drabbles

Book #3

The Monster Moves

Melissa watched the monster that killed her mother creep out of the kitchen and down the hall. The front door rattled and whined as it opened. Then it slammed shut with a BANG!

Melissa rushed to the living room window and peeked out through the crack in the curtains.

The monster's horrible, glowing smirk lit up a patch of darkness around it as it crossed the empty street. Slowly, in crept to the neighbor's lawn and slunk low against the ground. It squirmed its way through a crack in the wall and into the neighbor's basement. The monster's new home.

The Sleeping Cage

I never understood why my parents forced my brother to sleep in a cage in the basement.

They said it was to protect him. To protect us. I didn't believe them. I hated that cage.

It was abuse!

One night, I snuck down to let him loose. He slept peacefully.

Until I unlocked the cage.

He lept out, knocking me to the floor. His eyes were wrong.

Evil.

Then the rest of him changed.

This was my brother.

But at the same time… not.

My brother didn't have fangs, claws, or scales.

Maybe the cage wasn't so bad after all.

The Last Egg

For our science fair project, my friends and I hatched chicken eggs. It was fun, and going really well.

They started hatching.

We watched as one by one, the eggs broke open. Tiny yellow chicks covered in eggy goop struggled to freedom.

So cute!

So tiny!

So helpless.

Soon there was only one egg left.

As cracks formed on the shell, the chicks peeped loudly.

Crack!

The last egg burst apart. And dragon a rushed towards our chickens.

That's right.

A dragon.

It roared a tiny roar as it attacked our chickens, filling the room with terrified peeps.

And blood.

The Auction

She struggled as they dragged her on stage. She cried for help, but no one moved. In fact, most of the audience laughed.

Maybe we should have felt bad for her, this young woman crying and trembling with terror. We would've once upon a time. Back when we were human.

But that was just it.

We *weren't* human.

Not anymore.

I licked my lips. My tongue scraped against my fangs as I smelled her blood.

Then the bidding started.

"One thousand!"

"Two thousand!"

"Three thousand!"

"Five thousand!" I shouted, determined to win her. She smelled delicious. And I was thirsty.

The Thing at the End of the Rainbow

It was supposed to be a Leprechaun.

Everyone knew that. You followed the rainbow until you found its end. When you did, you got to keep the pot of gold.

If you could kill the monster guarding it, obviously.

It should've been easy.

A cute little guy in a green outfit. That was what the stories said.

Just one quick, clean shot, and I'd be rich. That was the plan.

it was supposed to be a leprechaun.

Not a troll.

A *troll* the size of a building with a club to match.

Needless to say, I didn't get the gold.

The Dream

Ever since I threw that penny down the well, everything I dream comes true.

Last week, I dreamed I had a sports car. I found one in the garage the next morning. Then I dreamed I could invisible whenever I want to. That's an awesome power.

Then I dreamed I met my favorite celebrity. I ran into them the next day.

It's been a good week.

Too good.

Guess the universe had to balance it out.

Yesterday, I dreamed I was kidnapped by devilish monsters. I'm scared to leave my house. Because I know I won't be coming back alive.

The Coffee Thing

She shuffled into the kitchen, her foggy mind focused on one thing, and one thing only.

Coffee.

She set up the machine and turned it on. Then she turned it on and leaned against the table to watch it brew.

Drip.

Drip.

Drip.

Watching it fill the pot was so hypnotic, she didn't realize something was wrong until it was too late.

An arm made of sludgy brown grounds creeped out of the top of the coffee maker. It flopped on the counter and started growing.

Growing.

Growing.

Until it was big enough to wrap its fingers around her throat.

The Monster and the Stepmom

"Let me out! I'll tell Dad!"

Judy laughed. "Go ahead. He won't believe you."

I cried. She was right.

"Please! I'm sorry! Don't leave me here!"

"You're staying put."

Her footsteps headed downstairs, towards the living room. I was alone.

But not for long.

I huddled against the door. Waiting.

A minute later, it came.

The vent monster.

Slimy, bloody tentacles rose from the air vent and flopped on the carpet. It hated when the door was locked. The tentacles crawled towards me.

I cried but didn't move. Why bother? She locked the door.

And there was nowhere to run.

Playing With My Hair

Something tugged my braid as I worked at my computer. I smiled but didn't turn around. My kitten loved climbing on the back of my chair and watching me type. She also loved playing with my braid.

It was only a little distracting, so I let her stay.

"Hi, kitty bean," I chuckled. "Did you need some company?"

"No…" a strange voice hissed.

My fingers went still and ridged on the keyboard. I lived alone. So who -or *what*- was behind me?

"I'm… hungry…"

"W-what do you w-want?" I whimpered.

"Your… Hair…"

I screamed as claws dug into my skull.

In Bed With Me

I smiled sleepily as the bed shifted under my husband's weight. A blast of cold air hit my naked skin as he lifted the comforter and crawled in next to me.

"Mmm," I mumbled and snuggled closer. "How was work?"

He didn't answer. I assumed that meant it wasn't a good day.

Ding!

Tiredly, I reached for my phone. My blood ran cold as I read my husband's text.

Hey, babe. Stuck working extra tonight. Be home real late. Love you!

If he was at work… Who… Or What was in bed with me? I was too scared to look.

My Zombie Daughter

She stands in the corner of the basement, growling softly.

She stinks. Her arm is gone. Maggots squirm across her rotting flesh. Strong chains hold her in the corner, but I know she'll try to devour me if she ever gets loose.

I know I shouldn't keep her. The other survivors would be so furious if they ever found out. A zombie in our midst? They'd happily use one of our last bullets on me.

But what else can I do? She's my daughter. My last family member. And zombie or not, I swore I'd always be there for her.

Giants and Farms

The world ended. Not with aliens, bombs, or Jesus coming back.

But with giants.

You know, the ones from the storybooks?

Yeah.

Those kinds.

They did the sorts of things you'd expect from humongous monsters. They smashed bridges, pushed over buildings. Crushes terrified people under stinking feet.

Then they took over, rearranging our world for their needs. Their first order of business?

Round us up and put us in farms.

That's right, they turned us into farm animals. Like cows or goats.

Except we don't get to go to the slaughterhouse. They like to eat us raw.

Bit.

By.

Bit.

The Blood Factory

Jessica trembled as the vampires stopped at her cage. They looked her over, consulting their files.

Jessica wanted to kill them all.

But she couldn't.

The vampires owned all the humans here. Fighting only made things worse.

"The test groups loved 1325B's blood," said the leader vampire. She tapped her pen against the cage bars. "We need more from it."

"We can't take any more blood. It's already giving the max amount."

"Any more and we'll kill it."

"True. But we *can* clone it."

"It'll be painful for it."

They all laughed at that.

"So?"

Then they dragged Jessica out.

Together

Together the things crawled through the darkness of the forest, dragging themselves towards the warm glow of the campfire.

The humans' camp looked so inviting. So full of warmth.

Of life.

Of food.

Slowly, they surrounded the campfire, lingering just outside the light.

The humans talked and laughed and ate, completely unaware of their danger.

Together, the things used the trees to pull themselves up. They towered almost as tall as the trees.

Together, they roared their hunger.

Together, the things stepped into the light.

The humans screamed.

Together, the things laughed.

Together, the things attacked.

Together, the things fed.

The Bigfoot Team

I laughed when my friends left on their expedition into the woods. They were looking for Bigfoot. How could I *not* laugh?

I laughed again when they came back, calling me and begging me to come to George's house.

"Get over here!" Wyatt begged. "You have to see what we found!"

I laughed the whole drive over. I expected blurry photos and samples of hair that would eventually turn out to belong to a moose or elk or whatever.

I didn't expect them to actually catch one. And I certainly didn't except them to bring it back in a cage.

What is it?

Two kids stand above me, staring curiously.

"What is it?" One asks.

"I don't know. A snake?"

"Snakes don't have long legs, dummy. It's some kinda lizard!"

I sigh.

What a know-it-all. Who lets kids go into the woods alone nowadays? Weren't all the parents scared of killer kidnapper or something?

"Maybe it's part scorpion. See the tail!"

"You think it's asleep?" the first kid asks.

I was trying to be.

"I don't know. Gimme that stick! Imma poke it!"

I open my eyes.

The first kid jabs me with the stick. I *wanted* to let them live.

Not anymore.

Invasion

It crawls up my spine, the tiny monster the doctors released into me. It'll help me walk again, they say.

I want that so badly. To walk again.

But not like this.

Not as part of their sick experiment. Not with an alien monster sharing my body.

Hello, host. A voice that isn't mine whispers in between my devastated thoughts.

"Get out!" I beg.

The doctors watch, but don't interfere. The alien monster makes itself more comfortable.

I like it here, it hums excitedly.

It helps me stand.

Then walk.

But I feel no joy. All I feel is invaded.

The Boring Old Statue

"Mom! I'm booooored!"

"We're not done looking at everything," Mom says. She tries to sound upbeat, but her tone and smile are wearing thin.

"But this is so lame!"

"It's art! It's good for you!"

I groan, but she keeps dragging me through the museum. Finally, she has to go to the bathroom. She leaves me alone to look at statues.

I sit on a bench and glare at a statue of a Minotaur. "You're the *most* boring," I grumble. I pull out my phone.

When I look up, the statue stands over me, swinging its sword down at me.

Mr. Carrots

Mr. Carrots.

My English teacher's pet. He came to school every day to hang out with us. A huge brown rabbit who loved nibbling on hay and posing for selfies with the students. I loved his twitchy nose.

I loved him.

Until he started torturing me.

Until I started hearing his sickly sweet voice in my head, telling me my worst fears.

I loved him less then.

Then he entered my dreams, showing me my fears and laughing as he hopped through blood.

My teacher loved the "creative stories" I wrote about Mr. Carrots.

They weren't stories.

They were warnings.

The Zoo of Magical Creatures

When the magical creatures were discovered, zoos, aquariums, and theme parks were the first to profit.

Commercials aired day and night boasting real-life mermaids and kelpies! Feast your eyes on the great thunderbirds of North America. Be the first in your family to hold a dragon hatchling! See a manticore up close! Come to the sea monster feeding at six!

It was fun and games and wonder. Until the magical creatures began to fight back. They didn't like the cages and tanks. They wanted out. They wanted their freedom back. And they were writing their message in big blood-red letters.

The Trash Monster

It floated in the middle of the ocean. Growing bigger and bigger. Stronger and stronger. Until it wasn't just a heaping pile of endless waste floating it the Pacific.

It was alive.

It was strong.

And it wanted things.

It wanted to reach the land. To meet the humans who had created it. To say hello. And say thank you for giving it life.

Slowly, it drew more and more garbage to it, getting even larger. Animals fled from it. Or they tried too. It was hard to flee an ocean filling with garbage when you couldn't walk on land.

Never Name It

It was sort of cute, this mutant creature they had created.

Two heads, one cat and one dog, sat on its shoulders. The body of a cute little corgi with the sweet toes of a kitty. A long fluffy kitty tail.

The scientists liked it, this strange, unnatural thing. It purred, played fetch, and knew twenty different commands.

They called it Frankie.

They shouldn't have named it. That was one of the biggest rules of experimenting on animals.

Never name it.

Never love it

Never care.

Naming it only made it that much harder when they had to destroy Frankie.

The Broken Glass

Crack.

A long thing line appears in my glass prison.

Crack.

Then another one.

And another one.

And another.

Until at last, the glass in nothing but a big, complicated spiderweb of broken glass, just waiting to shatter.

Slowly, I reach out and tap the glass with one, long claw.

The glass falls, crashing to the floor with me and all the water in my tank. I flop to the concrete, grunting in pain until my tail becomes legs, and I can walk.

I rise unsteadily and go to kill my captors. They'd pay for treating me like an animal.

Regular Citizen

I'm not a monster. Well, not *all* the time.

I'm just a regular citizen.

I go to work five days a week. I'm rarely late or sick. I pay my bills and taxes. I keep my home tidy. Every week I meet with my book club at the local library. I volunteer at a local soup kitchen twice a month. I eat right and jog three times a week.

I like to think I'm a good member of the community.

Except when the moon is full. Then I… I can't control myself. I lose myself.

And the werewolf takes over.

When the Dragon Grew Up

It started out so small and cute, my dragon. I fed him bits of chicken and pork out of my hand. I taught him to fly. I taught him to catch mice and rats. I taught him how to swoop down and scare raccoons out of the garden.

It was all going so well.

Then he got too big to eat rodents anymore.

I tried to keep up with his hunger. I bought chicken by the truckload. But it wasn't enough.

I hope the deer and elk keep him happy.

I hope he never finds out how good humans taste.

Pictures to Delete

She doesn't *want* to get rid of them. She loves them. But she has to.

The police are starting to ask questions. If they find these… She'll be locked up.

One by one, she deletes the pictures. She feels awful as her collection goes away. Forever.

The man in the flowered shirt.

The old lady in the pantsuit.

The girl with the puffy scarf.

The boy in the grubby sweater.

The baby in the purple dinosaur onesie.

The pictures of her kills. Her accomplishments. They had to go.

She laughed when she killed them.

She cries when she deletes them.

My Ex-Best Friend

Most people have nice, happy collections of photos. Baby pictures. Cheesy family photos. Photos of their sunburned selves on cheap-ass vacations. Cute pet pictures.

Not me.

I'm different.

What's the saying? Oh yeah.

I'm not like other girls.

My photo albums are filled with pictures of all the people I've killed. I'm proud of them. Of course, I had to print them and put them in a pretty album.

I like the ones with lots of blood. Red. My favorite color.

But my vert favorite photo is of my first very victim. My first drowning. My best friend.

Ex-best friend.

Weekend Plans

It's Monday. And like every other teenager, I hate Mondays. No one likes coming back to school.

But i especially hate them because every Monday, my English teacher makes us write about what we did over the weekend.

I want to tell the truth. But I can't. She'd get me in big trouble if I write down that I spent the weekend following my ex and hiding under her bed.

So I lie.

I say I watched a movie when I actually watched Maya. I say I baked cookies when I really stole Maya's diary.

I lied. I had to.

Better Her Than Me

My sister's body looked small in the shallow hole I'd dug. Bruises covered her. Blood coated the back of her head.

"Better her than me," I muttered.

Trying not to cry, I placed her doll in her cold arms. So she'd have company on her trip to heaven.

I'd go to hell when Dad finally killed me.

My phone buzzed in my pocket. I pulled it out to check the text.

You done yet? he demands.

Almost.

Hurry. I'm hungry.

I sobbed quietly and start shoveling dirt over her. I felt so guilty. But I knew.

Better her than me.

Back to School Shopping

I stare in amazement at the huge selection of back-to-school stuff. My kids rushed up the aisle, snatching up highlighters, pens, and colorful notebooks. My son grinned as he dropped an armload into the cart.

"Can I get a big box of crayons? Can I, Dad?" my daughter asked. She held up a box that claimed it held two hundred and fifty different colors.

I nodded, distractedly. My focus was on a big display of decorative duct tape.

Pink.

Rainbow.

Mermaid scales.

Dinosaur patterned.

I tossed the dino one into our cart. It'd be fun to use during my kidnappings.

They Didn't Know

Everyone thought it was fake, our Halloween House. They all paid ten bucks to get in. Hundreds of people came to see it.

They thought it was fake. So they loved it. All the blood, gore, and madness.

They laughed in disgust at the man who took a bath in human blood.

They cheered when the scientist performed painful experiments on humans subjects.

They squealed with delighted terror as the woman cut chunks off a screaming man and ate them in front of him.

They laughed at the woman covered in spiders.

They didn't know the truth.

So they laughed.

Boyfriends and Background Checks

I have a new boyfriend. He's great. He's funny and super hot. Great in bed. Recently, one of my friends suggested I run a background check on him.

"You can't be too careful!" she said as we sipped coffee together.

I nodded and promised her I would think about it.

She does know that I already checked up on her. I don't want my friend to think I'm creepy.

But I do background checks on everyone. Not just my new boyfriends.

Family.

Coworkers.

Even her.

Everyone.

The world is full of crazies. And she's right. You can't be too careful.

In the Shower

I know what you do in the shower. I've been watching you for years. I watch all my tenants when they shower.

But you… you're my favorite. I know so much about you. I feel so close to you when I watch you shower.

you shower twice a day.

You sing *Disney* sounds at the top of your lungs.

You hate shaving.

You use strawberry shampoo.

You write swear words on the glass.

I wonder what you would do if you knew I was watching? Would you be mad? Or would you be flattered by how much I like you?

Texts and Bleach

My phone buzzed. I flinched and glanced at it. The only person who ever called or texted me was Mom. And I couldn't ignore her.

Slowly, I picked up the phone and checked it.

There was a simple, three-word text.

Come help clean.

Great.

She'd made a mess again.

Reluctantly, I went to the basement. Mom was already there, scrubbing at a bloodstain. "Get more bleach. This idiot bled a lot."

"Right," I stepped over the limp body.

"Hurry! You know, we can't leave evidence."

I checked the cupboard. "There's not enough," I whispered.

"Then go get more!" Mom ordered.

Eva Wonders

Eva really liked her new job at the gas station. She grinned when her classmate Jordan came in.

He waved at her and made a beeline for the coolers.

"Are you okay?" she asked as she rang up six different energy drinks. He looked even more tired and twitchy than usual. And that was saying something.

Jordan nodded, avoiding her eyes. "Just been helping Mom clean. Had to get more bleach."

"Ew," she laughed sympathetically.

It wasn't until he was gone that she saw the reddish stains his sneakers left behind. It looked like...

Blood?!

What exactly were they cleaning?

Waiting

When will you be home? I text my son. He's so *slow*. He *knows* I'm in a hurry.

I'll need to punish him. To remind him how important speed is in these kinds of situations.

I glare at the dead body. It's sprawled across the floor. Now that all the life was gone from it, it'd lost its appeal.

Now it was just a mess to clean up and get rid of.

My phone beeps. It's Jordan.

Almost home. Had to get energy drinks.

Yep. He'd be punished. No one kept me waiting like this. Especially not for energy drinks.

Why Some Kill

Some kill for revenge. To get even.

Some kill for justice. To make sure people pay for their crimes.

Some kill for self-defense. They'll only kill if it's the only way to stay alive.

Not me.

I don't kill for those sorts of things.

I kill because I like it.

Love it.

The fight they put up. The screams they make. The light leaving their eyes. That's my favorite part. The light in their eyes going out. The thing that makes them *them* leaving their bodies.

It's intoxicating, having that kind of power over another person.

That's why I kill.

The Deadly Couple

They've been all over the country. They've killed people in nearly twenty states. The police are desperate to find them, but they're always one step ahead of them. It's a couple, the police and newspeople say. A young man and woman.

They lure people away into dark alleys and kill them.

Then they flee to the next state and start again.

They're one of the most deadly couples in history, they say.

I've seen the surveillance footage of the man. I know him. I used to date him.

Now all I can think is how that could have been me.

Books

His family thought he was weird. That his passion for true crime was just a phase. He was a teen, after all. He probably just wanted to look edgy.

"He'll grow out of it soon," his parents said.

His friends thought he wanted to become a criminal psychologist. They thought he wanted to study the people in the books. "He's gonna be on those crime shows someday," his friends said.

They were all wrong.

He wasn't reading them because he wanted to study the killers.

No.

No, he read the true crime books because he wanted to be those killers.

Pay for the Sketchy Shit

I know why people come here. It's a shitty motel, so of *course*, people don't come here for a relaxing getaway. They come here for sketchy shit.

People come here for hookers. People come here for cheating on their partners. People come here for drugs.

People come here with people who don't want to be here. People come here to sell other people.

And people come here to kill other people.

And honestly?

I don't care what anybody does here. Do whatever you want as long as you pay for the damn room, okay?

Just pay me, and we're good.

Too Pretty

I had to kill her. She was so pretty, our neighbor.

Too pretty.

What if my husband started to want her?! I had to make sure that he wasn't tempted away from me. I had to.

I was helping him stay faithful to his marriage vows. I was being a good wife.

She was too pretty! Don't you understand?!

This was the only way.

Come to think of it, the woman up the street has really nice hair and legs. Maybe I should get rid of her too. To keep my dear husband faithful.

You know, because I love him.

Running Out

I sorted sadly through the last of our food. Rice, beans, and two dusty cans of peaches. There was only about two more days worth of food left. And when it ran out… I didn't know what we were going to do.

My stomach rumbled as I put my share of the food back. My children had to eat. So I would go hungry.

The food was almost gone. The money was *very* gone. Even the water was running out. My children didn't know things were so dire. And no matter how bad things got, I hoped they never would.

Free To Go Out

I wait for them to go to sleep. Then I kill them.

One.

By.

One.

I go after the weakest first. I smother my son. I use a pillow. It's easy. Then I kill my daughter. I strangle her. It's a little harder to kill her, but I manage.

Then, I go to the master bedroom. My husband dies with a cheese knife in his gut. He's the hardest to kill. Not because I like him or anything sappy like that. But because he fights back hardest.

When they're all dead, I smile.

I'm free.

I can finally go out.

How Long?

I know I shouldn't do it. But it's the one thing that makes me…
anything. The rest of the time I just feel numb.

Maybe it's excitement? This thing I'm feeling?

I don't really know anymore. I just know it's *something*.

And I have to keep doing it.

What am I doing, you ask?

Stealing.

I guess it's not the worst thing a person could do. I mean, it's not
as bad as murder. And I'm not taking anything important. Just little
things. Candy, toys, or crayons.

But I do wonder… how long do I have before it stops working?

Can't Let You Live

"You don't have to do this!"

"Oh, but I do."

"Please! Just let me go!"

"I can't do that. I know you'll just run straight to the police."

"No! No, I won't say anything! I promise!"

"I can't believe that. You saw my trophies. You know I killed them"

"I won't tell! I won't go to the police. I'll leave town! I'll never come back!"

"I can't risk it."

"Don't do it! Please don't!"

"I have to."

"Ronda! Put the gun down. Ronda, please! Put it down!"

"I'm sorry. I do like you… I just can't let you live."

Bang!

I Love Science

I love science.

It started with those cute science fairs we had in school. Then it grew from there.

My experiments went from innocent titles like, "Do plants grow better when they listen to classical music?" and "Does mold grown faster on white bread or wheat bread?"

To "How much bleach can I inject in a person's veins before they die?" and "What is the loudest a person can scream?"

But by far my favorite science experiment has been: "How many tapeworms can a person have inside them?"

That was so gross and fun.

Did I mention I love science?

The Perfect One

I drive around the city for hours, looking for just the right person.
They have to be perfect. Otherwise, it won't be fun to kill them.

One man is too tall. So he gets to live.

One woman is too round. She gets to live.

Three different teens are too ugly, so they get to live.

As the night gets later and late, I worry that I won't find anyone.
And then…

I spot him.

The perfect one.

He sits alone at the bus stop, nose in a book.

Good.

I like sneaking up on my prey and surprising them.

Sodas and Popcorn

First, she makes sure no one is looking. Then she takes the bottles of sodas out of her bag. They look exactly like the ones on the store shelf.

But these are filled with poison. Horribly painful, fast-acting poison.

She quickly mixes them to the display, so there's no way to tell the poisoned ones from the safe ones.

Humming to herself, she goes on about her shopping like she hasn't just done something terrible.

She buys popcorn for her after-dinner snack. It will be so much fun to watch the news tonight. She always wanted to do something TV-worthy.

Favorite Colors

Everyone at school thought I was weird. But this morning real sealed the deal for me.

Our new English teacher asked the class to say our names and favorite colors. And to say why it was our favorite color.

Like always, the popular kids went first.

Fred liked blue and white because they're our school colors.

Mary liked green because it's the color of money.

Brian liked brown because his favorite food is chocolate.

Then It was my turn. And everyone freaked out. I said I liked purple because it's the color of a human spleen.

Should I have lied?

Sins of the Parents

Our daughter didn't look right.

The priests told me and my husband she was demonic. That we had to get rid of her. I didn't want to.

This wasn't her fault. It was our fault. We must've sinned terribly for God to punish us so, the priests said.

I didn't believe them, but one woman can't fight the church.

They said we had to abandon her, or face exile from the village. So we did, even though it nearly killed me. We left her in the woods to die.

Alone.

Frightened.

I didn't sin before, but I certainly did tonight.

Wrong

Ghosts aren't real.

I hate when people say that. You wouldn't be so quick to dismiss them if you could see what I see.

The dark shadows that follow you. The evil, grinning faces that leer at us all in bathroom mirrors. The tall, grey, soulless things that stroke your hair at night.

There's nothing after death.

People are wrong about that too. There is something after we die. Something dark, endless, and horrible. Something filled with pain and demonic monsters you could never fathom.

I wish I was wrong.

But I know where we're going.

And it's not Heaven.

In the Mirror

I weigh myself just like I do every Friday morning. I groan and resist the urge to break my scale. How could I have gained weight again?! Frustrated tears fill my eyes, but I won't let them fall.

"Oh, please don't be sad!"

I squeal and spin. I live alone, so who was talking?

"In here," the voice says.

Tap.

Tap.

Tap.

That sound…

It's coming from the mirror.

Slowly, so slowly, I turn to look.

My reflection looks dead and decayed. Her eyes are as dark as night. It grins at me. "I think you look great," It whispers.

My Second Shadow

It's been following me ever since I came back from the haunted forest.

My second shadow.

It mirrors my first one. But every day, it grows tall, its limbs longer, it's head bigger.

No one else has noticed it yet. Maybe no one else can see it.

But I know it's real.

I just don't know how to get rid of it.

I peek at it as I walk home from work. It smacks and kicks at my original shadow, clearly laughing at its pain.

Laughing at *my* pain.

I muffle my sobs. I'll have bruises when I get home.

The Ghost and the Clothes

"Why don't you ever hang your clothes up?" My roommate asks. We're on my bed, playing video games. "Your closet's huge!"

I pretend to be hyperfocused on the game. "Just lazy, I guess."

"But your clothes would have fewer wrinkles!"

"I'm not trying to impress anyone." My laugh sounds forced.

How could I even begin to explain that the day we moved in, I saw the previous owner?

He hung by his neck in the closet. He's *still* hanging there. I can't put my clothes in there. He doesn't like it.

I know better than to make a ghost mad.

Those Things

I am *not* scared of the dark. I'm twenty-seven freaking years old. I'm much too old to be scared of something like the dark.

I am, however, terrified of the things that live *in* the dark. Those… those are *much* more terrifying. Those are the things you have to worry about.

The cold, laughing things that want me to join them. The things with dead eyes.

Those things are why I refused to get out of bed at night. Even when I have to go to the bathroom.

Those things keep me up at night.

Those things, I'm scared of.

The Dripping

Drip.

Drip.

Drip.

It's an awful, constant noise, the dripping.

Drip.

Drip.

Drip.

I checked every sink and tub in the house. I checked each room's ceiling. But I didn't find anything. No leaks, no broken taps.

But still. Something *had* to be making that sound.

Drip.

Drip.

Drip.

It sounded like the noise was following me from room to room. How was that possible?!

Drip.

Drip.

I swallowed. Silence was worse than drips.

A slimy, and invisible hand gripped mine.

"Come swim with me," a voice whispered as the invisible hand pulled me towards the backyard.

And the pool.

Something's in the Chair

He was proud of himself. He just did his laundry for the first time in forever. It smelled so fresh and clean. He deserved a soda for this. Now he just needed to fold it all and put it away.

He dumped the clean clothes out onto his armchair and went to the fridge.

He frowned over the top of his root beer can at the pile of clothes. It didn't look right. Almost like it wasn't on the chair. Like it was piled on someone.

The pile moved, clothes falling everywhere. A shadowy shape rose and moved towards him.

The Lonely Ghost

I felt so bad for him. He must've been terribly lonely. I know I'd be, if I was trapped under a house for thirty years.

So I started visiting him.

Nothing crazy, just sitting by the crawlspace under the porch and chatting with him about my days at work.

The ghost liked the company. He started leaving me little notes in the mornings, scratched into the deck.

Hello.

Friend.

Friends forever!

It was cute. Until late one night, he crept from the crawlspace. And made his messages into promises.

"Friends Forever!" He hissed as he dragged me into the crawlspace.

In the Bathroom

It happens every midnight on the dot. My bathroom door slams. The lock click. Someone sobs and pleads behind the door, even though I know no human is there.

Then the dark, shapeless mass shoots across my bedroom. It crawls up the door and surrounds the knob. Then the doorknob rattles, like the mass is desperate to get inside.

Then the pounding starts.

Bang!

Bang!

Bang!

It beats on the wood.

The sobbing inside intensifies. "Please! Leave me alone!"

Then the door opens. The sobs become screams.

It's horrible, but what can I do?

How can you help a ghost?

The Supernatural Section

It's horrible and fascinating at the same time. I can't look away.

The ghost floats by a wall, silver and see-through in the dimness of its graveyard enclosure. Its body is skeletal. Its ears are missing. The eyes too.

Dark silver drips down and vanishes before it hits the floor.

Blood.

I grimace.

I know people have to suffer horrible deaths to become ghosts, but this is a bit *too* horrible.

My boyfriend squeezes my hand to get my attention. "Want to go see the penguins?"

I smile and nod, happy to be leaving the supernatural section of the zoo.

The Book and the Dare

How to Summon Ghosts.

That's the title of the book I need.

But you have to be eighteen or older to buy dark magic books.

I'm twelve.

I should go look at the kids' books. I should put this back.

And I do.

I *do* go back to the kids' section of the bookstore. But not before slipping the ghost summoning book into my backpack.

I know it's wrong to steal. I know summoning ghosts is super dangerous.

But I have to do it. My friends dared me to summon an evil spirit. And I never turn down a dare.

The Ghost-in-Law

My mother was a horrible person in life, and she's a monster in death.

Literally.

She died last week. Her body is gone. It's buried deep in the ground of the local cemetery.

Her body is gone.

But her spirit isn't.

She's still around. Judging me. Torturing me. Letting me know all about it when she thinks I've screwed up.

Like today. She took all the dishes out of the cabinets and stacked them in a pyramid on the kitchen table. Even left me a nasty note carved into the tabletop.

Not clean enough. Do it again, you lazy pig.

The Stealer Ghost

I like haunting this family. They're very forgetful, very disorganized. I can steal almost anything I like from them, and they don't notice.

I steal lots of stuff I like and hide it with my body under the basement stairs.

Shiny coins. My grandma gave me spare change when I got to visit her.

The toys from fast food kids meals. I always liked those.

And I steal knives.

I don't take those because I like them. I hate them.

I just don't want this family's kids to die the same way I did.

Stabbed.

Scared.

Crying.

Covered in blood.

In the Hall Closet

I'm playing hide and seek with my little cousin. She's seeking. I'm hiding.

She tried to tell me I wasn't allowed to hide in the hall closet.

"It's the rule," she said. "The landlord said we can't use it at all."

Which meant that I had to. I wasn't gonna let her tell me what to do. I shut myself inside.

It was dark.

Cramped.

Dusty.

I smothered a sneeze as my cousin shouted, "Ready or not, here I come!"

"And here I am," a voice whispered as cold hands wrapped around my throat, cutting off my screams of fright.

Midnight Mother

I cover my ears as the clock strikes midnight.

It's loud, our old grandfather clock. But that's not why I cover my ears.

I cover my ears so I don't hear my mother screaming.

Even though she's been gone for three years, I still hear her dying moments.

Every night, at midnight.

Her running footsteps.

Her body hitting the wall.

Her pleas. "No! Josh, don't!"

The sound of the baseball bat smacking her.

Her wails of pain among the cracks of bones breaking.

I sob into my pillow. When I prayed to have her back, this wasn't what I meant.

The Worst Thing Ever

I used to think dying was the worst thing that could happen to a person.

I was wrong.

It's not dying.

No.

The worst thing that can happen to a person isn't dying.

It's becoming a ghost.

It's watching your family go on without you. Watching them die and go to Heaven while you're stuck.

It's a special kind of lonesomeness and misery that not even haunting can fix.

You're trapped.

You're alone.

And it's *forever*.

And you're *dead*, so there's no way to escape it. You just go on forever, slowly becoming angrier and angrier.

Slowly becoming a monster.

The Death Game

"This is supposed to be fun?"

"Yes!"

"Really?"

"Yes!"

"Can't we just play Candyland?"

"No! We have to play the death game!"

"So... what do I do?"

"Go in the bathroom with the candle. Keep the lights off. Chant, 'come kill me, demon!' Then blow out the candle and turn on the lights."

"And it'll be right behind me?"

"Yeah!"

"That's fun?"

"Yes!"

I roll my eyes, but light the candle and step into the bathroom.

I chant the words. I turn on the lights.

I scream. There's a demon behind me. I try to run.

But it's too late.

The Last Man

The father was the last one.

Literally, the last man standing.

The rest of his family was dead at his feet. Killed by his hands, but not his mind.

That was all me. I took him over so I could enjoy the feeling of killing again. It was nice. I loved the feel of their blood on my hands. Well, the father's hands.

Whatever.

The point was, they were all dead.

The daughters.

The cousin.

The wife.

Now, all that was left was to kill the father.

I laugh.

I take over his body and lead him to the window.

The Dead People

My daughter's artwork is starting to scare me. She no longer draws cute little flowers or happy unicorns.

Now, all her drawings are of dead people. Bloody, mutilated people with horrible, painful injuries.

People I had killed.

But how could she know about my victims? They were all long gone, rotting in shallow graves in the woods.

My daughter smiles as she shows me her latest drawing. A boy drowning in a bucket full of his mother's blood.

"Why did you draw this?"

"They wanted me to!"

"Who?"

"The sad people. They want you to know they're waiting for you."

The Man in the Fire

I watch the fire crackle, thrilled it's finally be Fall. I hate the summer, so I'm always super excited when the weather gets chilly enough to have fires.

It's bright and cheerful. It makes such a beautiful orange glow across the living room walls.

Suddenly, the fire goes out.

I stare at the smoking logs in confusion. That's impossible, for a roaring fire to go out, just like that.

It roars back to life, but this time the flames are grey and shaped like a person.

A man holding a huge ax.

He steps out of the fire, ax raised.

Something's in the Trunk

I woke up to a flat tire on my car this morning. Thank goodness my neighbor let me borrow his car. I totally owe him some take-out. I sing along with the radio as I drive home.

Thump!

Thump!

Thump!

What was that?

Thump!

Thump!

Thump!

There it was again. Something clunks around in the trunk. I pull into a parking lot and get out to check.

I open the trunk and frown.

It's empty.

At first glance.

Then, out of nowhere, come hands.

Rotting ones that grab me and pull me in.

The trunk lid slams, locking me in.

The Red Eyes

They're always watching me. The things with the red eyes. They watch me from every shadow.

From under the bed.

From behind the TV set.

From under the door when I go to the bathroom.

From the darkness of the closet.

From the bottom of the stairs in my basement.

I try to keep my closet closed. That's where most of them stay. They like the darkest, creepies parts of the world.

It's why I avoid going out at night. I don't want those things to get me. I don't know what they are. And I don't wanna find out.

In My Sister's Bed

We'd been whispering for several minutes when the door opened and the light clicked on.

"Who ya talkin' to?" My sister scrubbed at her wet hair with a towel and sat on her bed. "What? What's wrong?" she demanded.

I stared at her in horror.

"What?!"

"Y-you were just here! In the bed!" I gasped, clutching my blankets tight around me.

She looked confused. "I was taking a shower."

"But... I was talking to you!"

She shook her head, looking concerned and frightened. "You couldn't have been."

I shivered. If it wasn't her... who had I just been talking to?

The House I Haunted

I used to haunt the house I died in. I used to terrorize the families every night until they moved out.

But this family… I don't haunt them. I just watch.

The mother who rules the house with an iron fist is so much more terrifying than anything I could ever do. She hurts them so badly.

Mentally and physically.

Every moment the family spends with her is worst than forever in Hell. Every dream they have is filled with nightmares. Dreams of her, no doubt.

Even I'm scared of her, and I can't be hurt or killed. Not anymore.

Back to my Body

I crawl across the floor, desperate to get back to my body. I know that I'm dead. I know I can't go back.

I keep trying though.

Behind me, the demons growl.

I glance over my shoulder. I wish I hadn't. There are so many of them. inhuman. Their eyes are full of evil.

I crawl faster.

"You… can't go… bbbacckkk…"

I reach for my own hand.

One of the demons grabs my foot. And even though I'm a ghost, it hurts.

They drag me down through the floor. Through miles of rocks and dirt.

Drag me down to Hell.

The Chickens

The chickens cluck, peck, and fight each other as they swarm over the rotting body. It's putrid, stinking.

Absolute disgusting.

But the chickens keep fighting. Keep eating. They're skeletal, these dumb bird. But their beady little eyes hold a dark determination to live.

Flies and other bugs scatter as the chickens peel back rotting skin to get the inside bits.

A slimy little bug crawls over my shoes, desperate to escape the mad pecking. But one of the chickens scoops it up, and it's just as dead as the body.

This proves it.

Anything is food when you're hungry enough.

The Ants

When I got lost in the woods and broke my ankle, I knew I was going to die.

I knew it was going to be slow.

Drawn out.

Painful.

I knew animals would eventually come to eat my dead body.

But I didn't know they'd start when I was still alive. And I never thought the first things to start eating me would be ants.

They matched across the ground A neat row of red dots. They tore teeny bits of me away, starting with a small cut.

It got bigger and bigger.

And do did the line of ants.

The Witch and the Worm

I can't close my mouth.

I can't fight.

I can't even scream.

I'm completely, utterly, one hundred percent frozen. The witch's spell froze me like this. I can't do anything but lie in silent terror as the worm crawls into my mouth.

It's slick and warm and slimy. It's disgusting.

Worms. My biggest fear since childhood.

I can feel it inching its way over my tongue. I can feel it creeping toward the back of my throat.

It slithers down, down, down my throat. All three feet of it, until it's settled happily in my stomach with all its friends.

Ticks

Everyone likes pets. Some people like dogs. Others like fish. My brother has a pet turtle. And my sister has a beautiful parrot. My mom and stepdad are thinking about adopting a cat.

My choice of pets is a little different.

Okay.

A lot different.

My pets are ticks.

Yep. Ticks. Those little blood-sucking bugs.

I like them. I don't know why. I guess they just fascinate me. The way they crawl up anything with their tiny legs. The way they hang onto people and animals so tightly. The way they swell up so huge.

I just think they're neat.

Bed Bugs

I was having a nice dream about flying when something woke me up. I lay groggily for a moment, confused. What woke me up?

"Ow!"

Something just bit me!

I jerked back the covers and turned on my phone's flashlight app.

My sheets were crawling with thousands of bugs.

Spiders.

Worms.

Horseflies.

Everything you can think of, it was there.

Oh god!

I jumped up, swearing I slapped desperately at my legs and stomach. Where had these come from?!

As I jumped around, my flashlight jerked around my studio. I froze.

It wasn't just the bed.

There were bugs everywhere.

Camping

I didn't want to go camping. (Who went outside in the wilderness for days with no showers or wi-fi for fun?!) But my boyfriend talked me into it.

It wasn't so bad during the daytime. We swam in the lake and cooked hot dogs over a fire.

But then night came.

It was too dark. The ground was too hard. And I couldn't sleep without the drone of Netflix documentaries playing in the background.

But the worst thing?

That would be the animals.

Specifically, the big animal creeping around outside our tent. It kept coming closer.

And it sounded hungry.

Locusts

They invaded yesterday. Came in a big dark cloud of buzzing so loud we had to cover our ears as we ran. There must have been billions of them coming at us all at once.

Too many to count.

Too many to stop.

All we could do was run for cover.

When they finally left, and we could come outside again, the gardens were destroyed. Everything nibbled away. Nothing left but twigs.

I felt numb as I stood there, taking in the extent of the damage. It was freaky. Everything... just gone. It would've been impressive if it wasn't terrifying.

The Lost Snake

My day was already bad from waking up late and a shitty shift at work.

Coming home only made it worse. My roommate's snake, Hissy, had escaped her cage again. And he couldn't find her.

"Help me look?" he begged through tears.

I did, though I didn't have much hope. The snake escaped so often. It clearly didn't want to live with us.

We searched the apartment, going slowly from room to room.

We didn't find Hissy. But we did find the little window in the bathroom cracked opened.

"Shit," I muttered. I hoped the neighbors weren't scared of rattlesnakes.

The Lepoard Seal

It swims round and round my hunk of ice. I want to move. I need to move. But I'm too tired to swim. I lay on my side, panting for air. I can see the shadow in the water every time it passes.

The ice justles, and I flap my wings, desperate to stay on.

The ice jerks again, harder.

Teeth sink into my foot. I'm dragged into the gloom of the water. A face appears in front of me, full of teeth and smugness.

As it finally devours me, I think of my mate and egg. They're doomed too.

Something's in the Kitchen

"Kids! Time for dinner!" I call as I finish setting the table.

They pause their video game, and they come into the kitchen.

"Yay! Chicken!" Luke cheers.

We sit and start eating.

Halfway through dinner, we need more napkins. Jacob goes to get them.

He screams as he opens the cabinet. I rush over. There's something big and hairy attached to his face. I scream too and rip it off him.

The thing flops to the tile and scurries away on eight long legs, pinchers snapping.

Oh, god.

That thing's loose in the house. And I have no idea where.

The Strange Sheep

She fed them every morning, her sheep. She loved them. They were cute and friendly. They greeted her with happy noises and friendly demands for pats.

But today was different.

Today, there were twenty-seven sheep. And it wasn't like they all suddenly had babies either.

There were just... more. This wasn't normal. These new sheep... they were wrong.

They were bad.

Her original sheep ran to her, bleating. These weren't happy bleats though. These were terrified.

Slowly, she opened the gate and let them out. Letting them run loose was better than making them stay in there with the strangers.

The New Pet

When his boyfriend told him he wanted a pet, he was fine with it. Everyone liked pets. He imagined them going to shelters and pet stores together. They would fuss over every little detail until they agreed on the perfect critter to share their home with.

He expected to bring home a dog or cat.

Maybe a tank and some goldfish.

This thing his boyfriend bought…

This wasn't a pet.

This was a monster.

How did he let himself be talked into this? From the safety of the kitchen, he watched his boyfriend enter the cage holding their new tiger.

Zombies and Spiders

There's something no one ever thinks about when it comes to the apocalypse.

How do you feed your pets?

I mean, the world is falling apart around me. Zombies run loose. Food is wiped out. It's only a matter of time before the water and electricity are gone.

But what about my pets? They need food.

We're currently in the basement. We're hiding from the zombies. I turn from the window and look at my pets.

I'm almost out of food for them. I try not to cry. I love them. But should I really risk my life for spiders?

Truth Dare or Hippo

It was stupid. We shouldn't have done it. I see that now.

we just wanted a great video for our TikTok account. Our fans wanted content, and we couldn't let them down.

So we did the only we could think of.

We started a game of Truth or Dare with them. It was funny at first.

But it got out of hand. Before we knew it, we were breaking into the zoo.

Specifically, into the hippo enclosure.

I never thought they'd be dangerous.

I never thought I'd be in jail.

Or that Chad would be in the morgue.

The Endangered Species

Tigers are almost gone, people say. They're endangered.

But I have some good news.

Tigers will survive.

And when everyone finds out what I've done, I'll be praised across the globe.

Because I've just released three hundred tigers into the wild.

Did you read that right?

Three.

Zero.

Zero.

Three hundred tigers, out in the wild. Sure, they're in the Appalachian Mountains, but my tigers are smart. They'll do just fine out there.

I've been breeding them in secret for years, getting them ready for this. I've even taught them to hunt.

They won't be endangered anymore!

Everyone will be so happy!

The Jellyfish

I'm enjoying a quick swim when I bump into them. A swarm of jellyfish.

"Crap!" I whisper in irritation.

One stings me. "OW!" I yell and kick hard in pain. Another one stings too. "Crap! Ow! Ow!"

I try to swim back, away from them.

But it's too late.

And there are too many of them for me to avoid completely

My craps and ows become terrified shrieks of terror and agony as more and more and *more* jellyfish surround me.

Stinging.

Stinging.

Stinging.

My vision goes blurry.

My head slips underwater. Pain takes over.

And the world goes black.

The New Hobby

I was so excited when my son finally found a hobby. It was so much better than him just sitting in front of the TV all day. Now he was checking books out from the library, and spending time outside.

Reading and spending time outside.

What more could a parent ask for in an age of internet and social media?

But soon, his hobby started making its way inside. That was less exciting.

The ant farm was okay.

And the crickets were actually kinda cool.

But finding a giant centipede in my bed? On my face?

That wasn't so cool.

The First Pet

The lady smiled at me as I cuddled the Yorkie I had just adopted. His fur was so soft.

"I love him already," I grinned. The dog licked my cheek.

"I think he likes you too," the lady said, smiling too.

I thanked her and took my new dog out of the shelter and to my car.

He really was cute. I did like him.

But I couldn't get attached.

Not when Chompy, my alligator was waiting for me at home.

I'd promised him a very special birthday dinner tonight.

And I couldn't disappoint him.

Chompy was my pet first.

The Fins

They circle the island I'm stranded on. Like hungry vultures.

If vultures were more than twice as big I was, swam, and had fins that made them look super menacing in the water.

I watch them from the beach.

I'm so hungry.

Thirsty.

And scared.

I'm scared of dying slowly, trapped here with nothing to eat or drink.

I don't want to die like this. Slow and drawn out.

Sure, the sharks will be scary and painful… but at least they'd be quick.

Slowly, I get up.

I walked into the water.

Then I swam.

Right towards those menacing fins.

My Worst Fear

I hate snakes. They're my worst fear.

My family went to a state park for our summer vacation when I was five.

I was bit by a snake.

It was so, so awful.

I almost died.

It's why I don't go hiking. Or even to the park. I like nice urban areas. Places full of people. Areas where the biggest, creepiest wild animals are the occasional rat or a flock of pigeons.

That's why, when my boyfriend asked me on a trip to the beach, I agreed. Beaches didn't have snakes.

No one thought to tell me about sea snakes.

The Sting

We're playing in the backyard. My brother digs in the dirt. I'm swinging back and forth on the tire swing. I'm thinking about going inside to get ice cream sandwiches when my brother screams.

I hop off the swing and rush to his side. "What is it? What's wrong?"

My brother clutches his hand and wails. "It hurts! Get mom!"

"Why? What'd you do?" I couldn't see any blood.

He falls back, scoots away from his dirt pile, and points with the toe of his sneaker.

I take one look at the little brown scorpion and run to find mom.

Her Roaches

She kept finding more of them. Every day, more and more. She should think they're creepy and gross. She should call an exterminator. That was what any normal person would do.

She guessed she wasn't normal, then. Because she liked them. She thought they were kinda cute.

So she started feeding them.

People thought bugs were dumb.

But she knew better. Bugs were smart. Her roaches were smart.

They knew she meant food. They didn't run from her anymore.

In fact, they swarmed around her every time she went to the fridge.

Because they knew: when she ate, they ate.

Flies

Flies.

I hate them. They're so small and buzzy and annoying. Constantly crawling all over me and buzzing around my head. I swear that they try and fly in my mouth and nose on purpose. Flies are disgusting like that.

I need to get rid of them. I've tried everything. Sprays. Flypaper. Even just plain, old-fashioned swatters.

Nothing works.

They still find their way into my house. I don't understand why they want in here so bad anyway. I keep everything so neat and clean.

Maybe it's my new friends. They've been really smelly ever since I dug them up.

The New Edition

He hummed his favorite song as he counted his pets' cages.

One for the King Cobra.

One for the Copperhead.

One for the Black Mamba.

One for the Eastern Diamondback Rattlesnake.

One for the Eastern Coral Snake.

One for the Tiger Snake.

And one empty cage on the end for the new snake he was getting tomorrow. An Eyelash Viper. He was so excited, it was going to be a wonderful addition to his collection. Eyelash Vipers were so bright and colorful. He'd spent hours online, looking at photos of them. They were pretty.

He couldn't wait to meet his.

The Danger of Smiles

I smiled at the Chimps at the zoo. I thought I was being friendly.

But the Chimps didn't see it that way.

They saw it as a threat.

They jumped the fence. They tried to kill me. They wanted to. But my husband pushed me out of the way. He got the brunt of the attack. His face was ripped off, his hands torn apart.

I was attacked too, but the chimps were shot before they could hurt me badly.

My husband died. He's my hero. He saved me.

But not my smile.

I haven't smiled since my husband died.

Fires and Flashes

After a long day of hiking and exploring, we finally set up the tent and campfire. Well, my wife and I did. The kids played tag.

Once it was all done though, we all relaxed together.

We ate dinner. The kids roasted marshmallows. My wife and I cuddled.

"Selfie time!" My daughter threw her arm around my shoulders and held up the camera to snap a photo.

The flash blinded us. Then we looked at the photo. My heart sped up, terrified by what the flash showed us.

All around us, outside the fire's glow, lurked a pack of wolves.

IV

The Bonus Drabbles!

Hello, readers!
I hope you liked this bundle of all 3 books in the Bites Sized
Horrors series!
While you're here, please enjoy these few bonus drabbles.

New Year's Resolution

January 1st.

New Year's Day.

It's my favorite holiday. More than Valentine's Day. More than Halloween. More than Christmas.

Why?

Because I get to start my New Year's Resolution.

I make the same one every year. I do pretty well on it too. But each new year I try to do better.

Every year I vow to rid the earth of more sinners. There are so many. But every year now for nearly a decade, I've gotten rid of at least forty. That's good, but this year, 2022, I'm going to do at least fifty.

I hope I exceed it.

Cheapskate

When it comes to me and my brother, my mom is super cheap.

She buys amazing stuff for herself.

But never for us kids.

Mom shops at fancy stores at the mall. Mine and my brother's clothes come from Goodwill.

Mom eats lobster. We eat noodles.

Mom gets botox.

And when my brother gets sick and stays sick, he doesn't go to the doctor until he collapses at school.

He needs special treatments to live.

But mom refuses to pay.

I always knew she was cheap, but I never realized she was *that* cheap.

Cheap enough to let him die.

No Emotions

Once upon a time, in a kingdom far away, there were only two laws.

Never Laugh.

Never Smile.

The king was a miserable man. He refused to let anyone else be happy. Anyone caught laughing or smiling died by his hands.

His laws worked. It kept his kingdom exactly how he wanted it.

Quiet.

Joyless.

It worked.

Until the unthinkable happened. He caught his daughter laughing.

He loved her. But not enough to bend the rules.

He gathered his subjects and strangled her. He cried as he did so. He hated it.

So he added a new law.

No crying.

Snow and Railroad Tracks

When I was kidnapped, I was terrified about what would happen to me. As I thumped around the back seat, I imagined the ways I might die.

Cooked and eaten.

Cut up and mailed to my parents.

Locked in a room and starved to death.

But this… I could *never* have imagined *this*.

My kidnapper took me out into the woods and tied me to old rusty railroad tracks.

Then he left me.

At first, I thought he wanted a train to kill me. Then it started to snow.

And I knew.

He wanted the snow to kill me.

Slowly.

The Knowing

Drip.

Drip.

Something drips. I can hear it. But I don't know what.

Drip.

Drip.

It's not the sinks. It's not the shower. It's not the hose outside. What *is* that?

Drip.

Drip.

It's loudest in the hallway. Finally, I look up. A dark red stain forms by the corner of the attic door.

The cord that pulls down the ladder swings. Daring me to go up. To *know.*

I don't wanna know. Knowing means facing. Facing means calling the cops.

And I can't do that to my beloved wife.

So I turn on music.

And pretend I don't hear.

Not Peaches

I step out onto the porch, hissing as my feet hit the concrete. Snow falls slowly, covering everything. I shiver and call my dog. "Come here, Peaches!"

It's late. I can't see beyond the bit of light from my open door. I can't see, but I can hear. Peaches barks and whines at something.

"Peaches!"

A shadowy form rushes for me. At first, I think it's Peaches.

Nope.

This dog is bigger than Peaches. Bigger than my car.

It charges me, teeth bared.

I have just enough time to scream "Peaches!" before the monster dog's jaws clamp around my middle.

Worse

Something scratches from inside the walls. At first I ignore it. The house is old. There has to be a rat or two, right?

But every night it gets louder.

Bigger.

I put my pillow over my head, trying and failing to block out the noise.

It's too much. Too loud.

All.

Night.

Long.

I scream at the top of my lungs, "knock it off!"

Suddenly, the scratching stops.

I sigh in relief, certain I've scared away the rats.

Then a voice whispers from inside the walls. "Sssorry."

I hug my pillow, trembling, terrified.

It's not rats.

It's something worse.

The Thing in the Mirror

She hated mirrors. Her friends assumed she was self-conscious.

But it wasn't that she hated the sight of herself.

She hated seeing the thing lurking behind her. A big, hulking mass of darkness with blazing yellow eyes. She hated how it smiled when she did look at it.

She shivered as she brushed her teeth with her eyes closed. A puff of stinking breath ruffled her hair. She squeezed her eyes shut tighter.

She *felt* it *breathe* on her.

Oh god.

She'd only seen it before. Now she was feeling it.

Not a good sign.

How long before it attacked?

Dinner

"Eat your dinner, Sweetie."

"But, Mom! I don't wanna!"

"No buts! You have to eat!"

"But, Mom! I can't!" I'm not picky. I always clean my plate. But this… I can't.

"It's not *that* bad," Mom snaps and pushes my bowl closer to me. "This is all we have. So you'll sit there until you finish it."

I stare down at the bowl of meat.

I almost vomit.

I almost cry.

I know we're broke. I know we're starving.

But that doesn't change the fact that this dinner used to be my dog, Fluffy.

I'm going to be here forever.

The Smell

The smell is coming from the fridge.

It's a litter box in a hot car. Rotten eggs. A broken sewage pipe.

I peek into the kitchen. I'm not supposed to go in there. Not even for water. That's what the bathroom's for.

Kitchen is for grownups.

But it smells so bad. Soon, the whole house will reek. *I'll* reek.

I creep to the fridge. I open the fridge…

And scream.

Mom is in there. Well… her *head* is. *Mom's* making the smell.

Blood drips everywhere. Mom stares.

She didn't leave me, I realize in horror. *Dad took her from me.*

A Note From the Author! :D

Hello, Dear Readers!

I hope you enjoyed this book! I love writing drabbles, and I had a lot of fun with them. Especially the bonus stories. I'm pretty fond of *Cheapskate* and *Dinner*.

:D If you did like the book (and even if you didn't) please consider leaving an honest review on Amazon and/or Goodreads. It's a big help to both readers and writers. :)

If you enjoyed these stories and want to check out my other stories, please go check out my Amazon page! I have lots of short stories, flash fiction collections, and even a couple of novels. So there's something for every horror fan. :)

Happy reading, everyone!

Love, Lennie! <3

About the Author

Lennie Grace writes horror short stories and novels and looks forward to sharing her love all things creepy and spooky with the world. She works two jobs now, but someday hopes to write full time.

Lennie loves to write fiction that focuses on dark and creepy things, but is extremely nice and non-creepy in real life.

She is a lover of books, reading, and writing. She enjoys reading a little bit of everything, but really likes horror, mysteries & thrillers, fantasy and manga. Along with reading and writing she also loves animals, coffee, pizza, and all things cute and cuddly.

She lives in Oklahoma in a home filled with books and family members, both human and furry.

You can connect with me on:

https://wordpress.com/post/lenniegracehorrorstories.home

https://m.facebook.com/LenniesHorrorStories

https://www.goodreads.com/author/show/19013373.Lennie_Grace

https://www.amazon.com/Lennie-Grace/e/B07Q3MBFYQ/ref=dp_byline_cont_ebooks_1